SATISAR

The Valley of Demons

SATISAR

The Valley of Demons

Ayaz Rasool Nazki

Vitasta
Let Knowledge Spread

Published by
Renu Kaul Verma
Vitasta Publishing Pvt Ltd
2/15, Ansari Road, Daryaganj,
New Delhi - 110 002
info@vitastapublishing.com
MRP ₹ 350

ISBN 978-93-86473-23-3

Typeset & Cover Design by Vitasta Publishing Pvt Ltd
Printed by Vikas Computer and Printers

PROLOGUE

The troops raided the house of high profile media man, Ahmad Jalil, in Srinagar.

They had been ordered by their major to teach him a lesson, so they handcuffed him, dumped him in a military vehicle and drove away. His house was ransacked and special treatment was meted out to his study—they burnt some of his books and tore others, and manuscripts of great value were thrown out of the windows. Some fell into the flowing waters of the Jhelum, and others got scattered all over the place. Later on, rag pickers collected sheaves of these papers from the nearby park. I followed them to *Babademb* junk market where they dumped their collection on a heap of books and manuscripts stolen from the migrant Kashmiri pandit's homes and purchased the heap for posterity and put it to print.

Kashyap drove his brand new car himself. He never liked the idea of having a chauffeur. Driving alone in Kashmir's countryside was a spiritual experience and he was almost in a mood of meditation, sitting quietly behind the driving wheel. Travel around in the charming surroundings of Kashmir he often did, and this evening he was returning after three days of hassles at his sprawling apple orchard near the apple city, affectionately nicknamed the *chota* London of Kashmir by the locals.

He had to see off the last consignment of fragrant sweet apples bound for the markets in the vast and sweltering plains of India. He also attended to the last rites—yes, he called them last rites as he believed that with autumn, every tree in his orchard entered into a state of suspended animation, to be draped gracefully in its white snow raiment for its annual burial a little later, and then reincarnated again the next spring.

Doing some pruning here, burning some dried leaves and dead twigs there, setting right a patch of fencing here, a bit of earth work there and, finally, spraying all the trees with a pesticide to prevent deadly scab which ate into his profits. Kashyap was happy with this year's returns; a good harvest, he thought.

He accelerated his apple red Maruti-1000 to full speed. He wanted to reach home before darkness fell, take a hot bath and then hit the bed to sleep off the day's labour. Finally, he took the turn off the main road and entered his estate, situated on the periphery of Srinagar city. The long driveway cut his estate into two and the tall poplar trees stood like guards in full attention as his car sped towards the mansion situated at the other end. There he was. At the first honk, his wife appeared in the porch and, as usual, she was at her charming best, ready to receive him. One of his servants ran behind the car and, even before it came to a halt, opened the door to help him out. He entered the porch, put his arm around his wife and both went inside to the warm comforts of their luxurious life.

He heard the ringing of a bell. It was the ringing of a telephone. Suspended in that luminal state between sleep and wakefulness, he ignored it for a while, and drifted back into oblivion. But it was there again, persistent and nagging. He could no longer ignore it. Someone wanted to reach him. He sat up in his bed, turned on his bedside light, reached for the telephone, and called out in a sonorous voice, "Hello."

For quite some time, there was no response and then, just as he was about to hang up, there came a deep voice, speaking in measured tones, pronouncing each syllable clearly.

"1 am Jaladbhava...I am Jaladbhava...I am Jaladbhava... Kashyap cannot be spared...Kashyap cannot be spared," and then the line was disconnected.

Kashyap did not understand a word. "Hello...Hello..." He continued to speak into the mouthpiece.

His wife, sleeping beside him, had got up by now. "Oh, come on. Must be some madcap not able to sleep and disturbing others. Darling, it is 2 o'clock; come sleep," she said, yawning.

They had hardly stretched their bodies when the phone rang again. Kashyap again went through the motions and listened to the taped message from the other end. Again, he stretched himself and sat up. It continued like this till finally he disconnected the phone and both of them snuggled close to each other and entered the valley of bliss.

Five days later, an innocent looking letter sent by post lay on Kashyap's table. By then, he had totally forgotten about the mysterious phone call he had received in the middle of the night four days earlier. The letter read:

Dear Kashyap

Our *Tanzeem* has learnt from highly dependable sources that you are trying to create hurdles in the ongoing movement for freedom. We have earlier also warned you but it appears you are bent upon mischief and determined to continue with your activities. It is therefore ordered that you be punished with death.

Yours Sincerely
Jaladbhava
Commander- In-Chief

The same day Kashyap and his family crossed the Pirpanchal range.

❖❖❖

The announcement over the public address system at Jammu Railway Station about the late running of Jehlum Express sent a wave of indignation among the scores of passengers who were waiting for the train. Sitting on the bench at the platform, both heard the announcement and, for the first time, the elder seemed to take notice of his very robust and extremely handsome companion who was dressed in jeans and denim jacket, and was clutching a black briefcase with his hands. The young man seemed to be the sales representative of some company and appeared to be gazing at a point far beyond his immediate neighbourhood, unattached, unconcerned. Turning, the elder one addressed him, "Where are you going?"

He too seemed to notice his companion for the first

time; with a start, he turned his gaze and replied briefly, "Delhi."

The elder wanted to strike a conversation, so he continued. "The train is delayed."

"Yes and you too go to Delhi?" was the response.

"No, young man, I am going beyond Delhi," said the elder and stretched out his hand, "I am Maqsood Shah, the carpet dealer."

The young man shook the hand held out to him and replied, "I am Budshah."

The elder was dumbstuck. "Budshah"? When he was a child, he had heard about "*Budshah*" and…and that was all. The young man seemed to read his thoughts and continued with a royal grace,"Yes I am *Budshah Sultan Zain-ul-Abidin*, the Monarch of Kashmir."

The elder was totally swept off his feet. How sad, he thought! What a fine looking young man, but nuts. The young man understood, "You do not believe me. Listen, I had come to visit the migrant camps at *Geeta Bhawan* and *Muthi* and now I go to Delhi to see for myself the plight of my people."

The elder was now sure that the man was crazy but he had to pass time, so he decided to play on. With a lot of reverence, he submitted, "Well, my lord! Will you please tell me—in what condition did you find your people when you visited the camps?"

Budshah thought for a moment and declared in a voice choked with emotion, "I am in search of my people but alas! I have not so far found even one person from my nation, neither here nor beyond those mountains." Having said this, he got up and, walking briskly, disappeared into the crowd of passengers on Jammu Railway platform No1.

❖❖❖

Mulla Tahir Gani Kashmiri sat in the open window of his house, which overlooked the Mar waterway. The exquisitely latticed wooden windows were wide open and a pair of pigeons sat perched on their top, basking in the morning sun. It was a usualy bright autumn morning. Outside, Mar was beginning to come to life. Boats carrying merchandize of all sorts were arriving at the opposite *ghat*. The buyers would soon flock to the *ghat* and the normal hustle and bustle would commence. Within an hour's time, the boat bazaar would be at its best. These boats brought fruit, cloth, earthenware, copper ware, sliver and even gold jewellery and ornaments. Gani sat there in his little window watching the *ghat*. It somehow pleased him—this traffic on the waterway with boats of all shapes and sizes. The bigger ones carrying rice, timber, fodder, or the charcoal from far off villages and the smaller ones, the *doonga*, with the boatman's entire family on it, and the *shikaras*—the multicoloured, delicate boats moving about like butterflies on the crystal clear water of Mar.

Gani had an important appointment for lunch. He had been invited by one of his admirers, none other than the Mughal Governor of Kashmir himself. Should he or should he not go. Gani considered. He led the life of a recluse and shunned the wealthy and mighty. He lived in his own world of poetry and was a happy, contented man. He had not married, had neither longings nor belongings and it did not matter who came to see him. For him, nothing mattered. He spent most of his time in seclusion, detesting any intrusion into his privacy. He had not many visitors to his house. Only some obstinate pupils who would not let go of him. But right now, he pondered over one thing only; should he go for that lunch? He looked out; the bazaar had picked up. The men with the merchandize on boats were shouting at the top of their voices, advertising their ware, calling out to the buyers; the buyers too had started pouring in from all the adjoining *mohallas*. Traffic on Mar was at its peak. Gani had no ear for the noise. He wanted to get up and close the window, but looking at the pigeons, he decided against leaving his post as his movement would surely disturb them. He waited.

He looked out again. Beautifully decorated *shikaras* followed by a dozen *doongas*. He heard the notes of music flowing to his window from one of the *doongas*. Yes, he could make out—a party was on inside it. The *ghat* now reverbated with a milling crowd—men, women and children; the hawkers, the women selling vegetables and fish, the boats selling fodder for the cows, tobacco for the *hookah* and fabrics for clothes. In this hustle and bustle, two boys appeared from a bylane. One of them carried a grenade, which he aimed at the passing security vehicle but the vehicle sped away. The grenade landed on the road and there was a big explosion. People ran helter skelter, hawkers' calls gave way to cries and shrieks and alarmed voices. Soon, everything at that spot seemed dead. Only a few injured men and women lay on the ground. The crowd had vanished! The pigeons perched on Gani's window had flown away. He stood up, stretched out his hands and shut his window.

❖❖❖

They had long and heated discussions on every subject. Kashyap had always been curious, inquisitive and restless, whereas his companion, Arjun, was serene, composed and calm. Kashyap did not take anything at its face value, not even the exalted word of their guru. He always questioned. The ultimate aim being: to perceive the reality—Om. But he always failed to comprehend the ultimate reality. Shakti? Shanti? Vibhinta? Power? Peace? Diversity? What was it really like?

Arjun, on the other hand, accepted every word of his guru as the ultimate revelation. For him Brahma, Vishnu, and Shiva were realities. Roles were assigned to each. Brahma was the ultimate fountainhead of existence, Vishnu sustained it, and Shiva caused all the upheavals.

Kashyap was never satisfied with this sort of dispensation. He thought of other possibilities.Why three? Why not one? He always objected to set theories, challenging them. His guru was always patient, ignoring his outbursts of suspicion and doubt. One day, after a really heated debate in the *pathshala*, Arjun remained behind even after all the pupils had taken leave of their master. He reverentially fell at the guru's feet and said, "Master! forgive him for he does not know what he says."

The guru lifted him up by his shoulders and with a luminous smile said, "Arjun, I am proud of Kashyap. He is the last hope of the Gurukul."

And now the last hope of the Gurukul was leaving the Gurukul in search of an unknown world. A world hitherto concealed from the human eye. A chaste, pure and virgin land. It had all begun with a discourse by the guru. He had talked of accounts he had studied in ancient texts that there lay a country to the north of the plains, surrounded on all sides by lofty snow clad mountains and all lush green, dense forests, shimmering waters, vales and dales. The Guru had depicted it as *Swarg* (heaven) on earth. Beauty personified.

The Lord having assembled everything beautiful, and then concealing it from the human eye. Kashyap at first thought that it was a myth. How could such a country remain hidden from the greedy human eye? But the more he questioned the guru, the more he was convinced that it was true. Such a land did exist! Beauty! That was it! Kashyap began thinking of a new concept. Couldn't the ultimate reality be beauty with all other attributes flowing from it? *Sundarta*, yes, *Sundarta Bhagwan hai. Satyam Shivam Sundaram*! The more he thought, the more convincing the concept appeared and more appealing too. Shanti, the peace, flows from beauty. Shakti, the power, attends on beauty with folded hands and Vibhinta, the diversity, is but a shade of beauty. Arjun and the trinity are misconceptions. Yes. *Satyam Shivam Sundaram*. As this new thought took hold of Kashyap, a new resolve began to grow inside him. He would go to Sundar Desh and see the lord in all His glory. That would be his moksha—to become a part, even if a miniscule one, of Sundarta, a shimmer, a wave of sweet breeze, a drop of dew, a petal of a flower or a particle of fragrant clay.

His friends, especially Arjun, tried to dissuade him. His Guru warned him of the impossibility of his mission, the existence of Jaladbhava, the demon king, who with millions of demons guarded the country from intruders. The long unending battle between Shiva and Jaladbhava and the stalemate that continued, but Kashyap listened to none when he listened to himself. He set out on his journey.

❖❖❖

The entire population had assembled outside the village, awaiting the arrival of the maharaja's officials. The old men with creased brows, each line depicting the pain and misery of centuries, young men and women in rags. The women trying hard to cover their bodies, a little flesh revealed through a hole in the garment here and some through a gash there, some with emaciated infants clinging to their dry and shrunken breasts; the children, the urchins with white fungus on their heads playing in the dust. This assembly of starving, half naked humanity was led by a flowing pheraned and immaculately turbaned Peer sahib and the equally well-groomed nambardar of the village.

The petty officials in the maharaja's service were there for the annual grain collection. This year, the villagers seemed to be fortunate as the officials had arrived on time. Last year, the entire produce of the village had remained stacked and had perished during the winter. The officials were to collect the maharaja's share (the lion's share) and if they so pleased, would leave a few bushels for the villagers. That was the procedure; they were, after all, at best tillers. All rights of ownership were vested in the person of maharaja whose forefathers had purchased this country for a sum of Rs 70 lacs. The deed implied that all lands, mountains, forests, waters, skies, wild game, the fish in the pond, the chicken in the coup, the lamb in the pen, the cow in the herd and men, women and children were the personal property of "His Highness, the Maharaja Bahadur." He was a kind man because in spite of the deed, he did allow a few morsels of rice to his subjects and regularly dispatched his men to every village to collect his share.

The riders could be seen from a distance. Yes, here they were. A sudden silence fell on the assembly of wretched souls. Shrieking infants too smelt the approaching authority and stopped shrieking. The playing children suddenly froze. The entire assembly huddled closer. Children clung to their parents; women took refuge behind their men. By and by the riders came closer, and finally reached the place. The Peer sahib and nambardar took a few steps, held the reins of the horses and helped the riders dismount. The officials announced that they were tired and hungry and the nambardar immediately announced that the grains were not to be divided today. The sahibs would rest. The gloomy faced men and women slowly departed from the place. The officials had already left for the nambardar's house, led by the Peer sahib in his royal best.

❖❖❖

Raja Inder Sen, son of Raja Sunder Sen, sat on his throne. The ministers, nobles and knights of the kingdom were in attendance, attired in their best, nestled into their seats. Scantily covered damsels appeared on the scene carrying wine and began gracefully to serve those present. The courtiers talked amongst themselves in subdued tones. Presently, a bevy of beauties appeared in the center of the court and bowed before the king. They were all court dancers, beautifully decorated from head to foot. The raja took notice and with a wave of his hand gave his permission to perform. No sooner had the raja brought his hand down, the feet of the dancers began to move to the accompaniment of the drumbeat and dozens of drums produced a deep rhythmic sound. As the full orchestra came to life, the dance, the music and the wine seemed to invade the senses of all those present. Every part of the gyrating, twisting, moving flesh seemed to issue a passionate call that no one could resist. Taking a cue from the raja, every courtier began to pull the approaching dancer to his lap and plant a kiss on her even as she tried to free herself and dance away. This seemed to continue endlessly till suddenly a roaring voice emerged from the throne. With a raised hand, the raja ordered attention. The moving bodies became still, the fingers on the strings suddenly froze and the melody remained suspended in mid-air. The raja looked towards his minister who dutifully stood up. "Yes, my Lord?" he asked.

"Begin the business, minister, the court's business."

"Yes, my Lord."

"Present the report, minister."

"Yes, my lord. The entire Kashmir kingdom continues to thrive on your bounty and your mercy. My lord, the air, water and the land are all free. There is peace everywhere. No controls. People, free and happy, enjoy my lord."

"Good, minister! Good! But what about...him?"

"My lord? Oh him, the heretic? Yes, my lord, Nand Gupt roams about in the kingdom, trying to spread his vile thoughts. But no one lends an ear to him. Says he, 'Do not drink.' Women throw all filth on his head. Says he, 'Do not fornicate.' Men stone him for that. People are happy with their wine, women and mirth, but my lord, the rural folk are hard to change. We have ordered correctives here and there."

As the minister concluded his report, a couple of soldiers holding a man in chains appeared at the court's door. Bowing in the customary style, they entered the court. The raja enquired as to why they were here and whom they had brought in. The captain explained that the man was found roaming in the vicinity of the palace and when confronted, expressed his wish to speak to the king. "We have for the sake of security brought him inside in chains to your court."

The king asked the man, "What have you to say?"

The man, with a miserable look on his face, spoke thus. "My lord! I am an ordinary citizen of your kingdom. All was well with my life. I lived with my loving wife, two children and my old parents. Only a few months ago, my mother died. My father, taking the benefit of the new regulations promulgated by our lord, entered my wife, and this has ruined my own life and the whole household."

Hearing this the raja broke into a wild laughter. All the courtiers and soldiers followed. They laughed and laughed till the raja suddenly stopped. All the courtiers and soldiers also stopped and the raja in a vile tone thus decreed: "He is jealous of his father. Put him to death before dawn."

❖❖❖

It was the lull before the storm. She ate what they fed her; she wore what they held out to her. She toiled from early dawn to midnight in the fields, with the cattle and in the house. She did not say a word. She was in fact in search of the word. This silence was now becoming unbearable. She knew it was going to tear her apart, burst her chest and destroy her whole being. Then, suddenly, it all happened. Sidh Baba appeared from nowhere. It was a full moon night and she was looking for a lost lamb on the plateau of Pampore. Saffron fields lit up as thousands of saffron flowers brightly shone under the magical spell of a full moon. She saw her guru levitating in mid-air, holding the full moon in his right hand and plucking stars from the sky with his left. She fell to her knees. "Tell me what do you want? And it shall be granted. All the wealth in this world, all the power of the kings and much more shall be yours."

"My Lord! Power to the kings, wealth to the wealthy but yoga to the yogini will suffice. Knowing the unknown and the bounty of the word may not to me be denied."

"Brighter than this moon, enduring than the stars—thy wish be met. To the within from the without you shall go and unravel and know that which is unknown. Word be thy wisdom, deed be thy seed, and eternal bliss harvest thine."

After this, Lal did not go home. She did not need to. In fact, she had acquired her own kingdom, where she could do as she wished. The necessities of mortal existence had become meaningless. From self, she was on her way to non-self. She roamed about freely, from one place to another, one hamlet to yet another, dancing in the lush green meadows, spread in the vastness of her being, flying like a sharika and singing hymns to her soul, discarding in the process her worn-out pheran; naked she was free of all encumbrances.

Serenely shrouded in her nakedness, she roamed. They saw her roaming amidst the thickest forest. They saw her towering head above the tallest Deodar tree. They saw her unkempt hair mingled with the clouds above the mountain peaks. They saw her marble whiteness, whiter than the purest milk. They saw her and her lovely nakedness shone. Her lovely nakedness shone in the darkest and narrowest of minds. Her nakedness inspired awe and reverence. People flocked to her. They clung to her naked being; they put their hungry lips to her full breasts. They were all her own children, and like a big hen, she spread her wings to accommodate her chicks on a cold and dark night. Lal, the mother, continued to roam, imparting the word to their lives.

Gani sat through the night, lost in the deep valleys of his thoughts. He was known for his eccentric ways of life. He did not bolt the doors and windows of his house when away, but religiously secured every door and every window the moment he was in. When asked, he would reply that people lock their houses to protect the wealth within, when they are away. Since the wealth in my house is Gani alone, why bother when Gani is away?

Though dawn was breaking and a faint orange streaked the horizon, Gani remained seated on the mat. He was thinking of Saib, the great Persian poet, who had recently visited him. Saib had come all the way from Iran to understand the meaning of a metaphor used by Gani in one of his verses.

"Each strand of hair in her plait is like the potter's thread, tearing human heads like pots from a potter's wheel." Saib stayed for some time with Gani and all the time listened to him with great reverence and rapt attention. This was a great honour for Gani, but he remained what he was, a totally detached, uninterested soul, with no longing and no passion for this world. A hermit contented with his life and at absolute peace with himself.

The sun had risen by now and a new day had dawned. Gani finally decided to end his night. Suddenly, tearing apart the serene silence, a raucous voice filled the space. It pierced the bolted windows and doors of Gani's house. "All members of the public are ordered to come out of their houses immediately and assemble at the nearby chowk. Anyone staying behind will be shot as soon as spotted. Hello...hello... members of the public...."

It went on and on and with it came the shouts of men, shrieks of women, wailing of children. All hell was let loose. There was a pounding at Gani's doors. Somebody seemed to be determined to pull it down. Gani got up, walked through the corridor steadily and without any hurry, unlocked his door, and found himself facing soldiers in full battle fatigues. "*Sala, tum kyon nahi nikalta... uloo ka patha.*" The soldiers hit him in his face. Some pulled him by the collar and shoved him out into the street. Outside, he saw others being paraded and shoved out from their houses likewise. The soldiers were hitting all and sundry with rifle butts and raining abuse on them. What was the cause of this sudden agitation, he wondered. He too joined the herd of men and women on way to the chowk. From a distance, he could see his philosopher and guide, Fani, being marshalled out from a street, his gown torn, his turban missing. He was bleeding profusely from wounds on his face. Seeing him, Gani yelled, "My master! What is this? Didn't you contact Dara? Has this state gone out of the domain? Who are these people? And what do they want?"

With an acid smile, Fani stopped him. "How many questions do you have? Dara? Telephone lines have been disconnected. And who are these bastards and what do they want? You do not understand! It is Aurangzeb removing Dara from the scene."

❖❖❖

The magnificent Partishiver temple stood majestically on the bank of Bhawan spring. A wide expanse of glistening blue water took on a golden hue as the first rays of the sun kissed the glittering pinnacle of the temple. The birds nesting in the trees around the place suddenly woke up from their slumber and began to chirp in unison. The door of the nearby dwelling was thrown open and two sadhus dressed in saffron, both carrying a trishul in one hand and a *kashkol* in another, appeared on the scene. Their long flowing beards and shoulder length hair gleamed in the morning sun. At first glance, they appeared to be twins, though a closer look brought out some differences in their features. Walking with all piety and humbleness, their wooden sandles made a murmuring clatter on the green stone tiles of the temple compound. As they appeared, birds chirping joyously in the nearby trees descended and waited like duty bound guards all around the place. By and by, the two reached the temple door, which they opened and proceeded straight away and headed for the sanctum sanctorium in the beautifully decorated temple hall. Once in front of the deity, both of them prostrated on the ground.

The jingling bells were heard all around and the people came out of their homes. This had been the practice through ages. Every man, woman and child would begin his day with salutations to the deity at the temple. The congregation grew in numbers and the routine rituals, which the two sadhus conducted with grace, got underway.

The day's routine puja was still underway, when a tall lean man in sadhu's attire appeared at the temple doorway. One of the two sadhus conducting the puja saw him and immediately stood up. This shifted the attention of the congregation to the visitor at the door. Eventually, the entire congregation stood up and with bowed heads and hands folded with great reverence, waited in silence. Seeing this, the man took big strides across the hall, even as the people made way for him. He reached the deity and prostrated himself in front of it. After a few moments on the floor, he stood up and moved towards the two sadhus. The entire congregation watched as the sadhus blessed the man. Then, looking at the crowd, the man in a commanding voice declared, "Today, have I seventy-nine years of my reign and hundred years of my life. Today, this kingdom do I renounce and to spend the rest of my life in the service of the lord, do I resolve. I hope and do beseech my gurus, Maruswamy and Haruswamy, to approve of this and also that Biasdeva, my own son, now ascend the throne."

Saying this, the great monarch, the warrior who had never tasted defeat and who had even followed his adversaries in hot pursuit beyond the seas, relinquished his monarchy. Raja Ram Dev sat alongside his two gurus in front of the deity and the congregation followed suit. They completed the morning rituals and people began to leave. Raja Ram Dev, escorted by his two gurus, left for the guru's cottage in the temple yard.

The Raja had decided to renounce the world and he had arrived at this decision after reasoning out every detail in his mind. It was not a momentary decision, taken in a flash of temper, or frustration. He had ruled for seventy-nine years. Brought up as a prince and having lived the life of an absolute monarch, could he shun this world and the luxuries that he was used to, so easily? Could he live without power as a humble servant of the lord? He had debated these questions for months before taking the final plunge. Squatting on bare ground in the guru's cottage and flanked by Haruswamy and Maruswami the new convert to a sadhu's life was lost in his chequered past.

❖❖❖

Away from the raja's palace, an old man with an arched back walked barefoot. His sole companion was a staff he held in his right hand. Shrouded by an ordinary cloak, the man seemed lost in deep thought. His march to the central square in the heart of the city was slow and painful. His body was so frail and weak that for each step that he took he had to lean on his wooden staff and rest a while. But the determination of his mind and spirit ensured that he finally reached his destination—the city square. This city square was the open-air harem, where games of the flesh began each evening at sunset. Men, women, of all ages, shapes, sizes and inclinations gathered here each evening to engage and revel in the vilest and most carnal of games emanating from an imagination that passion could ever inculcate. And all of it was by a single royal decree.

When Nand Gupt finally reached the city square, he was shocked out of his wits. He had not in his wildest dreams imagined that man could be so vile, and so mean. The square was bursting with all kinds of human shapes. Drunk they were and yet kept drinking; not an inch of flesh was covered. It was a nightmare that the old and pious Nand Gupt found himself in, a scene from hell. He had never seen human flesh paraded so shamelessly, the human spirit descended to such depths, morality evaporated so easily in an orgy; orgy of banal creed. The very foundations on which humankind stood seemed to have been removed.

Men and women, in pairs, in groups, men with men, women with women, youngsters with those old enough to be their parents and grand-parents, the stench of perversion overwhelmed Nand Gupt. He felt he had entered the kingdom of Satan. He could see Satan busy in his lustful dance. Suddenly, Nand Gupt became still and a gleam appeared in his eyes. Slowly, he summouned up the last ounces of energy still left in his old and worn out frame and perched himself on top of a raised platform in the middle of the city chowk. He looked like an elongated island, surrounded by a sea of human flesh. He cast a longing glance over this mass of nakedness and in a choked voice addressed the deaf.

"Oh, people of my city! Listen to me! Listen to me! You

are heading for disaster. You are heading for a catastrophe! If only you could see. Listen to me. Death and destruction shall visit thee. Listen to me. You will all vanish, not a trace shall remain. Thus, as I say it shall be. Listen to me."

Nand Gupt knew that he was addressing the deaf. His rhetoric was lost in the noise that emanated from the crowd. Grunting sounds, animal cries, piercing shrieks, words of mirth and wild laughter. No one bothered about him for no one existed there. He descended from his pulpit. But he was still determined to reach his people. He tried to shake every being into wakefulness but the entire crowd had become insensitive to his touch. A heavy curtain seemed to separate Nand Gupt from his people. For a long time, he tried—tried everything. But when he heard the distant roar of a thunder in the skies, he ran for his life, away from the twisted and mangled mass of flesh, away from the city square and away from the city itself.

❖❖❖

Mahaballi sent a message to Yousuf Shah requesting him to join the national mainstream and contribute sincerely in restoring the political process. The message clarified that all future deliberations would have to be conducted strictly within the limits of *Ain-e-Akbari*. Yousuf Shah was thrilled with Mahaballi's message. Breaking protocol, he called on

Birbal, who had brought the message, and invited him to his house. Birbal expressed his desire to taste a steaming Wazwan. Yousuf Shah immediately rang up the royal cook, Sultan Khosa, and ordered him to report. Sultan Khosa, on receiving the royal command ordered his men to load the copper ware in the waiting Matador van and drove off to the palace. Birbal was getting bored with all the waiting, so Yousuf Shah ordered Khatoon to prepare saffron kahwa. The lady replied that they had run out of all bakery items. Since kahwa could not be served alone, Yousuf Shah drove out immediately in his Maruti car to GN Bakers, where he was received with full state honours. While the items were being packed, he suddenly saw some people from the press and he began an impromptu and informal press conference.

From Delhi, Todermal announced that the government would never hold any negotiations with gun wielding militants and all accusations about human rights violations were false and meant only to lower the morale of security forces working under difficult circumstances. Todermal's statement was heard by the flying squad on the walky-talky fitted in the vehicle. The flying squad suddenly came to life and surrounded Yousuf Shah. He was nabbed without any resistance and straight away driven to Papa-2. In the company of militants, Birbal, reclining against a soft cushion and drawing from a beautiful *hookah* at Yousuf Shah's residence heard of the arrest on Doordarshan. But somehow they did not hear the Hindi news. Birbal promptly switched over to MTV channel as the remote control was with him. Madonna was raining and all the militants were thoroughly drenched. Birbal seeing that the militants were busy with Madonna, gave them the slip by jumping out of a window. It was very dark outside. He walked to the nearest lamp post and requested him for light. The lamp post told him "Yes, it is a fact. The light that Mohan Das saw in Kashmir is my legacy but the Udhampur transmission line has become outdated. Now, there is one way out—a political and economic package. If you can manage that, the bulb hanging from my head will come to life and under my dazzling light you can enjoy your Wazwan."

Birbal was happy to learn all this and he immediately started for the Qaf mountains. He knew that out there, on the top of a black mound stood the mouth of a cave, and within this cave lay the city of demons. Situated in this city was a palace—the Anand Bhawan—and this palace had 10,000 cellars. In each cellar, there were 110,000 iron cases. In one such case was the package shrouded with a red rag bearing a white plough insignia and it contained a pack of 52 cards and 370 gold coins. Birbal set out on his journey to get the 52 cards and 370 gold coins. He knew that once he had them he would win the jackpot at the casino in Delhi and could enjoy his Wazwan in downtown Srinagar.

❖❖❖

In a famous auditorium at Delhi, 'Kenun Kashmir' had organized a public meeting and a large number of Kashmiri pandits and their women had assembled. A good number of speakers were seated on the dais. Kashyap of Kenun Kashmir, in his inaugural address, dwelt in detail on the Kashmir question. He clearly brought out the Kenun Kashmir stand on various issues confronting the Kashmiri migrant pandits.

He strongly demanded a homeland inside Kashmir in which Kashmiri pandits could live a protected existence. It was to be like the Dachigam Hangul Sanctuary. There at the sanctuary, with financial help from international agencies like World Wild Life Fund, the threatened Hangul had been provided a haven, which preserved this near extinct species of deer. Kashyap argued that if such an arrangement could work for Hanguls, then surely it could work for Kashmiri pandits.

In the first row of listeners, detached from the noise that periodically rose from the audience, seemingly listening to each word spoken from the dais, sat a handsome young man. He was wearing a denim jacket and holding a black briefcase in his lap. One by one, the speakers spoke giving vent to their thoughts, detailing their plans and priorities, demanding action, relief, jobs, admissions in schools and colleges, promotions, flats, plots, etc. At the end, it was decided that the entire assembly of men and women would in a procession move to the prime minister's residence and submit a memorandum, listing all the demands that had been made. Consequently, the people came out into the street and began their noisy march. They raised slogans and appeared highly agitated. The handsome young man also accompanied the crowd silently. After walking awhile, the procession came face to face with the Delhi Riot Police holding batons and carrying tear gas guns. The officer on duty ordered the assembly to disperse, but the agitated men and women pressed on. The police swung into action and baton charged the processionists. A few tear gas shells were fired. A baton charge caught the head of the man with the denim jacket. A tear gas shell burst under his feet. He fell down on the road, unconscious and bleeding profusely from his wounds.

He regained his senses and found himself on a hospital bed, surrounded by police and medical staff. The doctor on duty, seeing him open his eyes, called out to the police officer in a bored voice. "Here...he comes. I think you can talk to him."

The police officer came closer to the man and asked in what sounded to his ears a very professional tone. "What is your name?" The young man looked at him for a while and answered in a royal accent, "Zain-ul-Abdin."

The police officer made an entry in the sheet of paper he carried. "What brought you to the procession of Kashmiri pandits?"

"My legs!" The young man replied with a mischievous smile on his lips. The officer then nodded to one of his men who presented a black briefcase. Pointing to it the officer asked, "Is this yours?"

"Yes, this belongs to me."

The officer turned round to one of his juniors. "We are right. He is a dangerous terrorist, a hardcore militant."Saying this, he began giving instructions for increasing the security around the hospital. The young man in the denim jacket had meanwhile closed his eyes and gone into a deep sleep.

❖❖❖

Accompanied by his wife and children, Kashyap arrived at Jammu. Jaladbhava had finally succeeded in throwing him out. Kashyap imagined the frustration Jaladbhava must have experienced in not finding him in the valley. He felt good. But it also reminded him of his plight—he, a well-to-do, wealthy, and respectable citizen had become a homeless migrant within a few hours—yes, all within a matter of some hours only. His mansion, his cars, his estate, the orchard and all other possessions were left behind. He had merely saved his own and his family's lives. He had to sort out many things; there was much thinking to be done. But let this initial shock be over. In any case, there was no way that Jaladbhava could be allowed to rule indefinitely.

It is a passing cloud; he comforted himself. I shall be back in my mansion, in my estate and in my orchard, and soon, Kashyap reasoned.

Standing at Jammu Bus Stand, Kashyap saw a multitude of men and women, children and infants arriving from the valley. Some one told him that Raja Jag Lochan had made immaculate arrangements to receive these people and house them at Muthi and Mishri Walla. Kashyap was now happy. He immediately hired an autorickshaw and started for Muthi. A huge number of men and women were already there. He became a part of this multitude. His own community, his own tribe. Really immaculate arrangements were underway. He asked an official on the scene, "Sir, why are you pitching these tents? Do you think we can live in them?"

The officer replied in a confidential tone, "Don't you know, this is where you will have to be for a fortnight and within this fortnight, Jag Lochan will bombard all the Jaladbhava's demons and the Swarg Dharti will once again come under your noble feet."

Kashyap turned this piece of just received information over in his mind. He did not mind spending few days in a tent, or even under the open sky. He gladly led his wife and children to the tent allotted to them. His wife was not impressed but Kashyap gave her a passionate hug and a long kiss and then in a hushed tone let her know, "Sweetheart, we shall go back and when we do, you shall have three mansions instead of one, ten orchards instead of one and I shall buy all the jewellry and all the gold that you desire."

❖❖❖

It was a 'crack down'. The armed forces directed the men who had been ordered out of their homes to fall in a line, and when commanded, move one by one in front of a parked vehicle. This was called an identification parade. An informer sat behind the smoked windshield of the parked vehicle and if a suspicious character passed, he would press the horn. The attending military men would pounce on the man and take him away.

Gani and Fani were in the queue. The line moved very slowly. Gani, looking at the men in the queue and the palpable tension in the air, was reminded of all the accounts of the day of judgement that he had read and had been told about variously—first by his mother when he was a child, then his elders in the family, later the mullah in the mosque and in sundry discussions with friends when he was already an adult. That is the day when, it is believed, all mortals will stand trial and be awarded with the entry to heaven or hell. The entire existence of these unfortunate people depended on the pressing of a button. Everyone in the queue moved with stone heavy feet. Fear was writ large on each face. Gani on the other hand seemed to have gone beyond all emotion.

He was not even angry with these uniformed men. In his heart of hearts, he sympathized with his fellow beings, but maintained silence as no one was allowed to speak. To him, these men seemed to have been transformed. They moved like mechanical robots, their movements being guided and controlled by the men in steel. Gani turned round his head to see Fani. There he was with an acid smile on his lips and fire seemed to emanate from his eyes, so furious did they glow. With his whole frame shaking wildly, he lifted both his arms up and high into the skies. Not a word did he utter, though his soul felt as if it would burst forth from him. The silence was defeaning!

Those in the queue saw him but remained motionless. Gani finally turned round to attend to his master. Noticing an agitated Fani, the soldiers ran. They began pushing and beating him and succeeded in separating him from the queue. The military men made a circle around him and with lathis and rifle butts began to thrash him. Fani, who till now could not utter a word, suddenly came alive. A thunderous laughter burst from his heavy frame. Laughter like the roar of a thousand cannons fired at once. Roar of a pack of hundred lions, a laughter reverberating and echoing all around, from each dale and each hillside. It went on and on, drifting, spreading throughout the entire chowk, till it reached the loud speaker fitted on the minar of the nearby mosque and was then amplified several times more and broadcast far and wide. The armed men ran in panic. They tried to stop this roaring man. They went on hitting the laughing man. Lathis and rifle butts and heavy boots rained down on Fani for what seemed to be decades. But Fani's laughter did not wane. The army men were getting frustrated. Gani continued to be in the queue watching his teacher, philosopher and guide, listening to him as he laughed and then suddenly—it stopped.

There was a deathly silence all around. It seemed as if the air too had frozen into stillness. The army men were relieved. They removed the pile of lathis and guns so that Fani's body could be recovered. But alas! He had cheated them yet again. There, under the heap of lathis, nothing remained. Fani had in his true style disappeared. The commanding officer ordered his men to conduct a thorough search for him. The armed men again converged on the queue of unfortunate men, asking each one "Who is Fani amongst you? Who is Fani amongst you?" The forces were again frustrated after a while. They went to report failure to their commander. No sooner had they done that, when the laughter rose yet again, across the valley, echoing all around, till after what seemed an eternity, a voice from somewhere behind the mountain peaks roared, "Commanding Officer! You are Fani!"

Gani later informed the Commanding Officer that in Persian, Fani meant mortal.

❖❖❖

She had been roaming all day, ascending hills and descending into beautiful valleys. Travelling vast flower bedecked meadows and crossing singing streams. The farmers ploughing their fields, the women carrying manure on their heads, the children merrily playing under the trees—all saw her as she approached. A flash of light, a shimmery breeze and a whiff of fragrance in their lives. They ran towards her, clung to her luminous being. "Mother mother attend to us," and she did attend to all of them, sharing their sorrows and their joys, listening to their tales of woes. A childless couple, a sick man's troubles, a meagre harvest, and too much rain—all these woes were told to her, and she lightened their burden, softly comforting them with hope. She was the messiah in their lives, roaming and reaching all mankind.

In a family, a baby was born, but alas, it would not suckle at its mother's breast. Lal came in, "Show me the child. Here you are. Nund has come. Nund shall rule hearts of men. Why do you shy away from a woman's breast, when shied you not while being delivered from her womb?"

"Come my child, hold my breast and drink from it, for you shall know all that is to know." The baby eagerly held onto the breast with his tender lips and suckled her dry. Lal got up and left the house for she had now to go to the river and look for a boat. She had spent her entire nectar on Nund who had sucked in the very last drops too.

"Who shall without profit or some gain help me cross the river tonight?" she called out. She came to the bank and saw at a distance a boatman rowing towards her. Lal, in a frenzy, ran away and reached a busy baazar lane. She went to the grocers, "Cover me, son; give me a raiment, naked I am." The grocer laughed and took it as a joke. Lal cannot be shrouded ever, the eternal moon. She went to the bakers. "Cover me, son; give me a raiment, naked I am." Before the baker could react, Lal went in and jumped into the leaping flames of his oven. The baker, fearing for his life, put a lid on the fire so that no one would ever come to know what had transpired. After a while the lid came off, and shrouded like a fairy in a white robe, Lal came out. Like the princess of some far away land. A bride bedecked in the most dazzling of ways. The baker baffled, asked thus, "Lal, what is this? How come thee needed to clothe, for all know, that always naked you have been?" Lal replied, "My dear son, a man today for the first time have I seen rowing a boat across the river I wish to cross.How could I, a woman, approach him naked and break the rules divine providence has approved of?"

Saying this, Lal departed from the bakers and proceeded towards the river bank. On her way, she saw the boatman coming for her. As they came face to face under a tall majestic chinar, they bowed to each other in mutual reverence. The boatman held out his hand and Lal held it with her own. Then both went towards the river bank, and descended seven steps to the waiting boat.

Men and women from all over the place heard of this and gathered at the river. Waving their hands, crying with joy, tears flowing down their cheeks, they bid farewell to their queen.

❖❖❖

There it was. The legendary Swarg Desh. Kashyap did not believe his own eyes. The valley lay spread out before him as he stared down from a mountain peak. He had toiled day and night for this moment in his life. Bruised, tired and utterly exhausted, he lay there watching the reward of his toil. Yes, there it was. Like an emerald encased in white pearls. The shining white snow clad peaks stood like sentinels guarding the treasure that lay at the bottom. The large expanse of shining blue water in the center of the valley reflected all the mountain peaks, all the thick forests and at first glance it appeared as if yet another valley lay beneath the water. Kashyap could not take his eyes away. The breathtaking beauty emanated from every tree, every blade of grass that grew within the valley. Kashyap, though exhausted and forlorn, felt a new surge of energy within him. He would descend into the valley before it was dark. He could not hold back now. Throwing all caution to the winds, the fear of Jaladbhava not withstanding, Kashyap began his downward trek in gay abandon. He was not bothered now. He had reached his destination; he had achieved in his lifetime his singular goal. Even if he perished now, it was not a bad bargain.

From the time Kashyap reached the top of that last mountain, his every movement was being monitored. Jaladbhava's mountain surveillance force had picked him up on their radar. The energy changes on that peak had been monitored at ten different stations. The anti-intrusion force was already on red alert and Jaladbhava was kept posted. He had instructed his assistants to allow the intrusion and ascertain the purpose behind. But for this, Kashyap would have evaporated on the mountain peak under a volley of missiles fired at him. But he, oblivious to all this, continued his descent. He was enamoured by flowers in full bloom. He had never seen such flowers before of all colours, and all shades. A sweet fragrance hung in the air and multi-hued birds sang in unison. There were fruit trees on the way and Kashyap was startled to see the variety in shape and size. He would pluck an apple, take a bite and feel transformed into another world. Passing through a dense expanse of forest, Kashyap could sense the presence of a variety of game. The richness of flora and fauna really startled the man from the plains.

By and by, Kashyap's descent was complete. He reached

the bottom of the valley and proceeded towards the bank of the lake, to what seemed a lush green meadow, with hundreds of flowers blooming at every step. The sun was fast descending behind the western mountains. "It will be dark after sometime," Kashyap thought, but he wanted to see the sun set and enjoy every bit of this heavenly atmosphere.

He sat on the green emerald turf facing the west and waited. The orange coloured luminescence was spreading on the western horizon. The snow-clad peaks appeared to take on a golden hue and the rays of the setting sun danced over the blue water in front of Kashyap. This really was Swarag Desh, no doubt about that. Suddenly, Kashyap recollected Jaladbhava. 'Where was he? Could he be in his abode under the water as the legend goes? Or was he concealed in those dense woods? Where could he be? How could this beauty belong to him? No, I must not allow this, even if it means a fight. I shall destroy him with all the power at my command. I will not rest until I have freed this land from those who claim it as their own.'

The sun was about to disappear behind the mountain peak and it was beginning to get dark. Kashyap, lost in his own thoughts, continued to sit on the emerald green sheet of turf.

❖❖❖

Nund Gupt ran like one possessed. He had abandoned his staff. The arched back had straightened out and his legs were moving at a tremendous pace. After every hundred strides, he would stop, listen to the passing wind and look at the sky above in a terrified way, and hearing the distant thunder, resume his run. He was going away from the city, heading straight towards the Zabarwan hills. Running madly, he passed several hutments and small villages on his way. Then, as a he approached a sleepy village, he heard the cries of women, shrieking women, "Who is crying? Who is shrieking?" He had cried out.

His marching feet brought him into the village square. There it was—all hell let loose. He could see parked military vehicles, and then beyond men in chains tied to the trees, women being dragged from their huts into the square where soldiers, like mad wolves were tearing their flesh. Nund Gupt stopped silent and stoned.

Women, women. Ah! women. Miserable women. Young and old women.Women, the first to suffer.

Nund Gupt spent the last of his tears and ran away—away from the men, away from the present, away from the past, away from time. Near the foot of the hill, he again halted; listening to the distant roar and seeing the clouds gather up in the sky, he began his ascent. The gush of energy seemed to wane. His march slowed, as step-by-step he negotiated the difficult terrain, falling here and jumping there, but continued with his uphill climb.

The clouds had thickened and a light drizzle was at hand. He had smelt rain in the passing breeze. He wanted to reach the peak of this hill before dark, for he knew he could not walk in the dark. With a renewed vigour, he resumed his ascent. The rain began to fall faster and faster, and as he was half way up the hill, it came down in torrents and gales. Drenched from head to foot, the frail old man continued to walk, avoiding the rocks and the thorny bushes.

By the time he reached the top of the hill, the rain had assumed monstrous proportions. He could not see anything now as a continuous sheet of water fell from the skies. Nund Gupt looked up towards the sky as darkness fell all around him. He lifted his hands up and began to pray, "Oh lord of the skies; Oh lord of the lands; Oh lord of the seas; Oh lord of days; Oh lord of nights, I pray only to thee, hold thy wrath, for they do not know who have gone astray; Oh lord of the heaven! I pray to thee! Take pity on their souls! Harm them not, for they do not know. Oh lord of the skies! Oh lord of the land!" Saying his prayer, Nund Gupt prostrated himself and remained in supplication.

It rained all through the night and the following day; in all it rained for forty days and forty nights. On the morning of the 41st day, when Nund Gupt lifted his head, he saw a clear beautiful blue sky. He thanked his lord up in the skies, and then lowering his gaze, he searched for his city. There lay a vast expanse of clear blue water in front of him.

❖❖❖

The maharaja's officials had been camping in the village for the last four days. They had spent all the time in enjoying the hospitality of the village nambardar, eating the best cuisine, with dozens of natives in attendance. They seemed to be having the time of their life. They had been to the nearest forest in search of game. But the purpose for which they had descended on this village remained unaccomplished. The division of the farm produce had not been undertaken, and that meant continued starvation for the village folk, who anyway had got used to the miserable existence. On the fourth day, the village headman had arranged a musical feast for the officials and Maqbool Dar had been summoned to be there with his band for the concert that evening.

Maqbool Dar was a village bard who wrote his own songs and sung them too. He had raised a band of his own and it had achieved a good degree of public acclaim in the area. People loved him for his songs, his clear and youthful voice. He would play almost all the musical instruments with considerable ease, but the *matka* was his favourite. To him, it was like playing with the simultaneously chaste and voluptuous body of his beloved, his fingers caressing her lips, playing at her neck or merely touching her bosom. He was a master in his own right but somewhat eccentric in his ways.

One more day, Maqbool Dar thought as he carried his *hookah* to the nearby stream, filled it with fresh cool water and returned to his hut. Setting it in front of him, he placed the tobacco in the *chillum* and picked a few embers of charcoal from the kangri and placed them on the tobacco. His *hookah* was ready. Squatting, he looked out of the window. A new day had begun. Drawing the first puff from the *hookah*, Maqbool Dar thought, 'Is this day any way different from yesterday or will tomorrow be any way different from today?' That was the question. This nation had lost its struggle for existence. For centuries, its days had been the same—monotonous, drab, and filled with drudgery and misery. Nothing was to happen. Nothing was to change. Nothing could happen. They had been condemned to this sort of existence. Maqbool Dar often thought that his cow was better than him. Even the dog in the street lived a more decent life than him and his fellow beings.

He deliberated on these questions and these ideas were reflected in his poems. The beloved in his songs was in fact not a woman of flesh and blood. He did not sing to a charming maid. He did not lament the separation from the tormenting damsel. He, in fact, sang to his country, lamenting the days that had been beautiful and bountiful. He prayed and beseeched his beloved to smile upon him. The fairy was in fact the fairy of destiny, which, it seemed, had been cross with him and his people for some sins or misdemeanor on their part.

Maqbool Dar had been called upon to sing today and sing for none other than the maharaja's men. If they approved of his songs, then may be they would give him a hefty *bakhsish*. Maqbool Dar reflected on these possibilities and continued to smoke his *hookah*. Suddenly, a thought flashed in his mind. Yes, today could be different from yesterday if we do not care for tomorrow. Let us not care for tomorrow. But how can today be different from yesterday? Could it be? Yes, indeed, it could be. Maqbool Dar seemed to have unravelled a mystery. He seemed to have unlocked a jigsaw puzzle. And in doing so, he suddenly became afraid of his own thoughts. Maqbool Dar! What is going on in your mind? Are you possessed? Maqbool Dar! Arise and go to Peer Sahib. He will give a taweez and also the benefit of his holy breath. No, Maqbool Dar! Why are you scared? Today can be different from yesterday and this can be proved.

He left his window and his hut. He straightaway went to the hut of his friend Ajab Malik. Together, they took a walk towards the village shrine and there they met their third companion, Lassa Khan. Together, the three of them hatched a conspiracy against the state. An act of defiance was thus planned.

❖❖❖

Raja Ram Dev, accompanied by his two gurus, was on his way to the deep woods. He had come to realize that in all the hustle and bustle at the Partishiver temple, it was not possible to meditate with single-minded devotion. They had set out in search of a cave, about which it was said that it was almost inaccessible and hidden from the human eye. Raja Ram Dev walked barefooted in the company of his gurus. The three men were similarly dressed in the traditional saffron coloured robes and carried identical *trishuls* and *kashkols* in their hands. They walked silently, negotiating the boulders and thorny bushes they met on the way.

Raja Ram Dev was lost in deep thought. He was amazed to realize that on the Lord's earth, one had to search for a place for establishing communion with the Lord. He was deep in thought; the day his father had died arose in the deep crevices of long held memory. His father had been a kind-hearted king. Ram Dev had taken over the reins of the kingdom at a tender age, but eventually, it was quite correct to say that, overcoming all odds, he had done well. He had spent a lot of his time in looking after his subjects. He felt pleased. He had established many new cities and towns.

He built hundreds of temples, and finally with the construction of the Martand Shiver, a dream had come true. He had toiled for years on this architectural marvel, calling craftsmen from far and wide. At times, he had feared that he would not be able to complete the Martand in his lifetime but at the end he had succeeded. Free from Martand, Raja Ram Dev was attracted to the idea of enhancing his power, conquering new territories, humbling established kingdoms and creating a vast empire. He raised a big army and set out on his conquests. The initial victories created an aura of invincibility. Dozens of Rajas surrendered without a fight. Be it Punjab, far away Bengal or Kannauj, no one resisted his advance. Raja Ram Dev, walking in the serene cool surroundings of his valley, suddenly found himself in the scorching heat of a battlefield. He saw himself leaving behind a trail of destruction, death and misery. He felt surrounded by thousands of dead, wailing women and crying children. He heard the clutter of fast moving warhorses; he felt all the dust and smoke rise to his eyes. He was stuck in those days of his past when a mere mention of his name would bring down powerful kingdoms, when his approaching feet would set cities on fire. He continued to be haunted by these memories. What is life, he had asked. Why all this violence, he had questioned. And finally he had given it up all. Why should there be wars? Why should peace not be eternal? He had approached his gurus and they told him that violence and war were based on greed and greed was in itself a sin.

'Moh Maya' was a web, and once in, no one gets out; there and then, Raja Ram Dev had decided to cast away this net. Come out of this maze and begin a new life in the company of gurus and pursuit of the Lord, he had commanded himself. The Lord to him was Shanti—peace—peace of mind, peace of the body, peace of the soul, peace of mankind, peace of animal life, peace of vegetation, peace of the elements, peace of nature.

But even after casting away his royal robe, peace had seemed far away, beyond his reach. Where to find peace? Peace is the Lord but where is the Lord? Not in *Moh*; was it in the sadhu's *kashkol*, in his *trishul*? Or in the helplessness of a child whose parents were killed in war? Or in the miserable widow whose husband had been ambushed? Or in the handicapped father whose son had fallen in battle?

This life and death question appeared really complicated, and to solve this single question was the fiercest of all battles that Raja Ram Dev had ever fought.

Lally Tigress, as she was popularly known, had assumed dangerous proportions. She was the self-styled commander-in-chief of a militant outfit "Dukhtaran". She was a special pain in the neck for Col Sharma, for she concentrated all her activities in the areas falling under Sharma's control. He had a dossier on her prepared by his field intelligence and leafing through it, he became increasingly intrigued. An impressive record, he thought. Born in a noble family of aristocratic lineage, Laila Dorabi was well educated. From her early childhood, she had evinced keen interest in religion and by the age of ten, she had memorized the entire *Quran*. She had studied Islam in great detail and while still in her teens, had begun delivering sermons to groups and gatherings of women. A graduate with a sound background of current affairs, she was naturally drawn to the movement. She established her own outfit, the Dukhtaran, which became the female equivalent of all the established male militant groups. She had received her training together with a hundred hardcore followers, all young girls, fired by religious zeal. She made her presence felt when she led a group of burqa clad girls and demolished all cinema hoardings in the city protesting against the use of women as sex objects.

This was followed by imposing a ban on the sale of cosmetics for women, and a call for observing the veil. The response was unimaginable. The very next day, ladies of high society were found donning the veil all over the city. Her writ seemed to run large. This emboldened her and she moved on to more dangerous areas.

She began her activities in the movement by providing shelter to the fighters, helping them as couriers and guides within the city. But after a while, she fired the first shots on a security vehicle, causing extensive damage. There was no turning back after this. Her girls were highly motivated, indoctrinated to do or die. Col Sharma wanted to know more about her. For instance, where did she ordinarily reside? But the dossier he had on her was incomplete. The field intelligence had merely recorded its inability to gather all such information as no one was prepared to risk it. Col Sharma thought that to be incredible. The lady seemed to be invincible. A way had to be found; she had to be eliminated and her gang had to be busted as he was under tremendous pressure from his superiors. Kill her or catch her was the only command he had received, but no one had hinted how he was to achieve that. That was the problem in Kashmir, the Col thought. Those sitting in AC offices in Delhi did not or could not understand the ground realities. Or they simply did not care to.

The telephone bell interrupted Col Sharma's thoughts. He lifted the receiver. "Yes, Col Sharma here. Yes, oh yes, go on. Good, where? Airport? When...second flight from Delhi? Good. Excellent job. Thank you. Okay." Col Sharma replaced the receiver and stood up, picking up his cap, checking his revolver. Then, he briskly moved out and went straight to his command room. Taking charge, he yelled instructions over the wireless. "I want a full team immediately and the entire area sealed. Urgent. I will see you at the Airport. Okay."

Having ordered the mobilization of forces, he sped away in his bulletproof vehicle, followed by a string of vehicles carrying soldiers. They headed for the airport. This was going to be the catch of the year, he thought as he negotiated the last curve on his way. At a distance, he could see an aircraft hovering over the runway.

❖❖❖

Squatting on the emerald green turf on the bank of a great expanse of water, Kashyap was in deep meditation. He had come to this valley in search of the Lord and here he was about to realize his dream. He had already sensed His presence. He knew he could attain his *moksha* in this country. His *samadhi* was suddenly disturbed. He opened his eyes. Hundred of torches were directed at him. He felt blinded by the light. He closed his eyes and after a while opened them slowly. He could now make out his surroundings. Behind every torch stood a being, helmeted and in full battle dress. Presently, one of them came forward and coming close to Kashyap commanded in an authoritative way, "Get up and follow me". Kashyap had no alternative but to do as he was directed. No one touched him. All the soldiers marched in unison, in a loose circle around him, while he followed their leader. After a while they stopped. One of them approached Kashyap and bringing out a piece of cloth tied it tightly over his eyes. Blindfolding him, they resumed their march. Two men held him by his arms in order to help him find his steps. Kashyap counted the first few steps but then lost count and gave up. Presently they came to some place for now they walked on smooth ground, till at last the march ended and Kashyap was made to sit and take rest.

After a while his blinds were removed and he found himself in a princely suite with painted terracotta tiles on the floor and paneled ceiling. The walls were adorned with pictures of lovely deer and golden fish. He seemed to be alone in the room. Some fruits lay in front of him and some cooked fish on the side. Though hungry, Kashyap was in no mood to eat. He was thinking about his plight. Who are they? And what do they want? They could possibly not be Jaladbhava's demons as they looked like human beings. Well, this could also be *Mayajaal*, which Jaladbhava had resorted to, only to deceive and confuse him. The door opened and two men and a woman appeared. The woman carried a wooden box. One of the men came close to Kashyap and put his hand on his head. The other man helped the woman open the box. They brought out a small round mirror from the box and the lady carried it to the man who had been holding Kashyap by the head. She handed over the mirror to the man who brought it close to Kashyap's face so that he could clearly see inside it. The lady went back to the box and tapped it thrice with her hand. A murmuring sound issued forth from the box and Kashyap looking inside the mirror was aghast. In the mirror he could see his entire journey from the time he had reached the last peak. This was really a magical world, Kashyap thought.

After sometime the lady again tapped the box thrice and the sound ceased. She took away the mirror and replaced it in the box. The man came closer to Kashyap and asked,"Now tell us what brings you here? Remember we will know if you lie." So Kashyap told them of his desire to see the Swarg, and how it was that this desire had brought him to the valley. The two men told him that the king would decide his fate.

Suddenly the door to the room was thrown open and many men with their heads bowed entered. They carried in a golden throne. As thy entered the room, the throne was placed in the centre. The men then took their positions around the throne. In a moment a majestically decorated person with royal features and bearing entered. A hush fell all around and the men bowed in silence as the man ascended the throne. Kashyap was totally dazed. He did not know how to react. He got to his feet and reverentially bowed before the seated man. With a wave of his hand the man on the throne acknowledged him and then directed him to remain seated. As Kashyap took his seat the man on the throne addressed him. "Stranger to our land! What brought you in?" Kashyap murmured in response. "I would like to know who has blessed me with his royal presence."

"Oh yes! You have not been told. I am Jaladbhava, the absolute monarch of this land and you have intruded into that land. Who are you and why are you in front of us?"

"Majesty! I am thrilled to be in the presence of a great monarch like you, but believe me sir, I was told that you...." "That we are demons? We know that you have spread this canard only to discredit us in your eyes. By doing that you wish to deny us this land that is, has been and shall remain, only ours. But who are you and why are you here? You seem to avoid a direct reply?" said Jaladbhava." "No, my Lord! I am totally relieved on listening to your Lordship. Now I have no fear. I know I am at the mercy of a just and kind king. Sir, I am a Brahmin and was a student when I heard of your great kingdom. The beauty, grandeur, and the bounty—together they aroused in me a mad desire that I should visit it before I die, in order to know, that which is unknown, in the true spirit of one who pursues knowledge as life's only concern and pursuit."

"Well! We are impressed by your frank answer, but did you know not that the one who enters this land shall never go out alive? You are wise with the word. Now tell us what you want? We shall not permit you to stay here in our land, even if you have a noble cause."

"My Lord! I shall not ask that which I know thou shall not grant. I only wish to stay awhile in the country, for I do not want you to break the golden rule that says that this land shall remain chaste and pure as long as it remains away from human greed. I only wish you to grant me leave to be here for a few weeks."

"And that we gladly grant to you but you shall go the moment told, or else you shall have to die."

"Yes my Lord, I am blessed. The king shall ever rule the hearts of men and preserve the pure world till eternity."

The king Jaladbhava got up and acknowledging Kashyap's profuse salutations, left the room with a smile on his lips.

❖❖❖

They called for ten able-bodied young men of the village. The plan was unfolded to them. While Maqbool Dar was to sing that evening at Nambardar's place, the entire village would be led to the nearest forest. Maqbool Dar would, during the course of his singing, instruct the youth to go and loot the stored grain and carry it to the forest and the ladies there would light a fire and cook the rice.

As evening approached, Maqbool Dar, having attended to the minutest detail of the first act of defiance, dressed in his Sunday best. Then, accompanied by his singing troupe, he made his way to the Nambardar's place. The officials were already seated and eagerly looked forward to a memorable evening. Everything was in place. Maqbool Dar tried his magical fingers on the pitcher and taking this cue, his companions began playing with the strings. Music—sublime, pure and chaste filled the room and the instruments took on a life of their own. Maqbool Dar's melodious voice rose from the depths of his soul and echoed in the valleys beyond. His audience fell into a trance, transported to another world, a world of total bliss. Maqbool Dar continued to play on his earthen pitcher, his men continued to beat the strings and his voice continued to float all over the place. Lassa Khan had been instructed to clandestinely add some opium to the food that was being prepared for the guests. Taking a cue from Maqbool Dar he withdrew from the room and proceeded to the kitchen. There the cook welcomed him and offered him a *hookah*, which he gladly took. After a while, when the moment was right, he brought out some powder and put it in the nearest dish. Ajab Malik was waiting along with the youth outside the house. As the dinner was being served to the honoured guests, Maqbool Dar thought the time was ripe. The heavenly music together with the heavy and opium-laced meal would soon produce the desired effect. In a few words cleverly composed he ordered his men to go to the stores and carry away rice—as much as they could. Ajab Malik supervised the whole operation. In a swift action they decamped with ten bags, full of quality rice, and after some time joined their womenfolk at the top of the hills.

Maqbool Dar, seeing the last of his audience slump down in deep slumber, stopped singing and quietly left the room, heading straight for the forest where he found the women busy cooking a meal.

❖❖❖

Raja Ram Dev and his two gurus finally located the legendary cave. Its mouth was hidden behind thick woods and a big rock stood at the top of the mouth leaving only a crevice open at the bottom. But it was large enough to allow a person to crawl in. The three of them went in and were astonished to see the world inside the cave. They found a long winding tunnel with wider areas interspersed here and there. A flicker of light made its way into the cave at every turn in the serpentine body. That was incredible! How did these rays of light manage to pierce the mountain and the woods on top? A steady supply of fresh air was also maintained and Raja Ram Dev and his two gurus were really happy to discover this secluded spot where they could sit in *samadhi* and attain communion with their Lord.

Presently the three decided to return to the Partishiver Temple, settle things there, make arrangements for routine chores and come to the cave for a long stay. As the three came out of the cave, the sun was beginning to set behind the lofty mountains. Raja Ram Dev and his gurus took hurried steps. They wanted to return before it was night.

After having come half way, they decided to take a short break and rest for a while. As they sat on the flat rock, talking amongst themselves, they suddenly found a dozen young men, armed with AK -47 rifles surround them. One of the men ordered them to stand and raise their hands. They did as they were asked. A few boys came forward and frisked them.

"Nothing on them, commander," they said. "Okay, blindfold them and take them to the base camp. They must be men from RAW."

Blindfolded, hands tied behind their backs, they were paraded down the hills.

❖❖❖

The informer seated in the green gypsy was carefully observing every face that passed in front of him. Even if the slightest suspicion rose in his mind, he would press the button on the board. As soon as the hooter sounded, the soldiers would pounce upon the person and drag him away, dump him in a waiting vehicle and drive him to the nearest torture center. At times these centers would be temporarily set up at a stone's throw of the search, and the people would be made to witness the entire sequence that finally led to the agonizing death of the person concerned. As soon as Gani came in front of the vehicle, the informer sitting inside got suspicious. The character in front was unique with a big turban on his head, in a flowing robe. He could not take a risk. He pressed the button and immediately. The attending soldiers pounced on Gani and took him away.

The commanding officer came to the informer.

"Well done my boy! Who is he?"

The informer was now at a loss. Who was he? Did he fit the description of someone known? Who was he? He considered for a moment and suddenly yelled, "Gulbdin Hekmatyaar."

That was it. The commanding officer halted the parade and lifted the siege. The prize catch was enough for the day. This was an enormous feat! They had arrested the dreaded Hekmatyaar himself. Armoured cars were lined up. Gani was placed in a bulletproof vehicle in the middle of the column and driven off to Papa-2.

The officers were congratulating each other, bursting with joy. Detached from all this sat Gani, centuries away from the guns pointed at him, in a torn gown, multiple wounds on his body, his turban in shreds, and lost in his own world, the absolute monarch of his own kingdom, murmuring to himself.

❖❖❖

Todermal in a hurriedly convened press conference announced the arrest in the capital. Giving details, the minister claimed that the terrorist had been arrested after he was wounded in a procession led by activists of Kenun Kashmir. The terrorist had close links with the ISI and he had planned to create havoc in the capital by causing RDX explosions at a number of sites. Many incriminating documents had been seized from his possession, and these documents clearly proved beyond doubt the involvement of a neighbouring country in destabilizing India. When asked about the nature of these documents, the minister disclosed that these documents were written in some ancient script and a team of experts had been constituted to decipher them. The team had its first meeting and decided to constitute a sub-committee with the specific purpose of undertaking a visit to the Pyramids of Egypt to reach a conclusion as to the hieroglyphic relation of these documents with the writings in Mohenjo-Daro. The sub-committee had been asked to submit its report in six months time, after which the team would finalize its main report within one year.

In the meantime, Budshah was allowed to leave the hospital. He was seated in a police van and as the van left the hospital premises it was preceded by a dozen and followed by another dozen armored vehicles. The convoy sped along the Delhi roads, hooting sirens and bringing the entire traffic to a standstill. Budshah sat quietly looking beyond his immediate vicinity. He was totally cut off from the hustle and bustle around him. He had been considering a particular issue. While in the hospital, he was highly impressed by the professional competence of the medical staff. The care with which these young girls nursed his wounds, the equipment available for treating diseases, and the overall working of the health care mechanism had forced him to take notice. Somehow, he wanted such expert surgeons and physicians, dedicated nurses and other hospital staff to be available throughout the length and breadth of his kingdom. How to do that? He had been considering these issues. He wanted his country to become disease free, a healthy, joyous, happy, prosperous nation. He resolved to take every necessary step in this direction.

The column of vehicles continued to run on Delhi roads till finally it reached a red granite fort. Budhshah was asked to come out of the vehicle. The men escorted him inside the fort and after walking through, what seemed to him to be miles of corridors, he was finally made to enter a room. There was a single rope cot lying in the middle of the room.

Only a single ventilator adorned the wall, near the ceiling. An iron grill was securely fitted to this ventilator. Budshah could only see a patch of blue sky through this gap. Fresh air was scarce. He felt hot and humid. He removed his jacket and placed it on the rope cot and seated himself on a corner of the cot. Suddenly, he felt all alone. The chain of his thoughts had long ago broken. His escorts were nowhere in sight. He stood up and went to the door, placed his hand on the handle and pushed. The door did not move. He pushed harder. Nothing happened. He pushed with all his might but the door refused to budge. For the first time it dawned on him that he was finally under arrest.

❖❖❖

Through that fortnight Kashyap remained glued to the pocket radio set that he had managed to take with him when he escaped from the valley. He eagerly awaited the news that Jaladbhava's men had been wiped out from the face of the valley. The idea of bombardment had not appealed to him in the beginning for it was sure to destroy his mansion also. After all, how does a bomb know that the house down there belongs to Kashyap and not to Jaladbhava or, for that matter, how does the fire, which was sure to follow any large scale aerial bombardment, know which was his orchard? It was sure to be destroyed but Kashyap and most of his companions in the tents were prepared to sacrifice their properties for the sake of Bharat Mata's honour in the hope that this would finally make them the only rightful owners of the entire valley.

As the fortnight passed, nothing of the sort expected happened. Yes, there were reports of large-scale arrests, killings and curfew, but the end was nowhere in sight. Kashyap became restive. How could he live in a tent for the rest of his life? Something had gone wrong somewhere. His immediate concern was his own and his family's upkeep.

The relief provided by the authorities was alright but how long would it last? Kashyap finally decided to act. He had to do something profitable. In an alien land what could he do? Start a business on his own? No, that would not be wise at this stage. Then what? He continued to ponder this question and finally as a flash of lightening an idea struck him. Property agents. Yes, that was it! From the very next day he began his new venture. "Kashyap and Sons. Property Dealers. Sale and purchase of plots".

Kashyap was soon to realize that he was an excellent broker. He would arrange a deal between the seller and the buyer and earn a neat commission in the process. No investment and no risk. Within a short span of one year Kashyap had come to be known as one of the most successful brokers in town. He had sold and resold hundreds of residential plots. His economic standing had registered a dramatic upswing. He again moved in a car and purchased a modest house in one of the fast developing colonies of Jammu.

While Kashyap was engaged in fighting his own battle for survival, his orchard at Chota London deteriorated. In the absence of proper care, the fencing gave way, cattle moved in and when the trees bore fruit the village children had a field day. His mansion at Srinagar mysteriously caught fire and Kashyap promptly filed his insurance claim.

❖❖❖

The entire airport area had been brought under siege. Col Sharma placed his men at all strategic locations. The runway, the path leading from the runway to the airport building, the arrival lounge, the luggage conveyor, the doors, each place was teeming with soldiers. His man Friday, the informer, was placed behind the glass door at the arrival lounge entry. He was to signal the arrival of the lady, the moment she crossed the door. The aircraft came to its final halt on the tarmac. The stairs were thrown down and the doors opened. Sitting there like a big bird the aircraft began emptying its contents. Men, women and children started coming out one by one and walked leisurely across the runway towards the arrival lounge. And then finally she appeared! There, at the top of the stairs, holding an infant in her arms. Dressed in traditional shalwar kameez, she wore a bottle green knee length coat. Her hair was neatly and tightly held back and covered by a green scarf. A young man, bespectacled, and wearing a business suit closely followed her. Both of them walked side by side, smiling and talking to each other. There was no trace of any anxiety on her face as she crossed the automatic door and the informer raised his cap for Col Sharma who looked from a corner of the lounge. He was surprised for a second. A baby in her arms! Something seemed wrong. Was it really a baby or a trap? He quickly tried to sort it out. Anyway, he took brisk strides and directly approached the couple. He stood in front of her.

"Hello young lady? How was the journey?"

She stopped, opened her mouth to say something, and then looking quickly around the lounge, smiled and said, "Thank you, officer. The flight was superb."

Col Sharma moved closer and almost whispered into her ear,"Lally, no chance—wisdom lies in giving up."

And that was the confirmation that Lally had been waiting for. In a swift move she snatched away the service revolver of Col Sharma from the holster where it was hanging by his side and in the same move brought it up and positioned it on his temple. "Now move!" she thundered. The Col was stoned into submission. Everything had happened so fast that he could not move a finger. She kept him at a safe distance and then handed over the baby to her companion. Free from the baby, she held on to the revolver with both her hands and commanded the Col to turn and raise his hands. He had no choice. A commotion had broken out all around. The soldiers with their automatic weapons watched in a stupor. What could they do? She forced the Col to a corner and stood guard, watching every little move in the arrival lounge. She ordered all civilians to one side and soldiers to another. Col Sharma's informer—a local in civilian clothes—tried to move from the door towards the passengers on the far side. At that moment Lally ordered him to stop.

"Don't go there. You do not belong to us. Come here and be in the Col's company." Then turning again to Col Sharma, she said, "Col, I can very easily walk away from here but be at ease I have no intention of spoiling the hard work you have done. I will gladly come with you. But I have only a little work to do before I call this off."With this she turned her gaze towards the passengers watching her in awe.

"My dear countrymen, with my arrest, even with my death the Movement shall not end; it shall go on for God the Almighty has ordained thus. It shall go on, as His writ is the only one that runs. We do not seek power, position, or wealth; we only seek that which is our right. The usurpers shall have to vacate our beautiful land and we shall run our own affairs in the true spirit of peace—Islam. The spirit that we believe in is the only creed. The creed of Allah as taught to us taught by his messenger—to him be peace. I only wish to tell you that many of you shall today fall if I fire a single shot from this gun, and that I do not want. I shall rather give up myself than bring any harm to you for it is for you that I fight. So I am going with him but before that I shall kill a man. His death is ordained thus, for a traitor has no right to live. There he goes," and with a swift move, she emptied the entire revolver into the chest of Col Sharma's ace informer.

As he fell in a pool of blood, Lally threw the revolver into the waiting hands of Col Sharma saying, "Officer I am sorry for the hold up! Come, let us go."

❖❖❖

Birbal reached Delhi and from the airport he straightway drove to Todermal's office. Storming into his chamber, Birbal burst out, "What the hell did you mean by getting Yousuf Shah arrested when I had succeeded in bringing him around? You did not even bother about the wazwan he was arranging for me."

Todermal smiled saying nothing but Birbal persisted and demanded a reply. Finally Todermal gave in.

"Look, son, wazwan is now available in Delhi also. No need to worry on that account. Yousuf Shah was planning secession. How could we allow that? He had no business in talking to Miss Robin Hood. National security can never be put to risk and then the moves we made were cleared by Mahaballi himself, so why not ask him."

Birbal could not argue after that for Mahaballi could not be wrong. Anyway, he wanted to pursue the Lamppost line and in right earnest start for Kohi Qaf. He went to his own office and called an assistant who was well versed with geographical matters. It was he who in fact had shown him Kashmir on India's map, when the department for Kashmir affairs was brought under his charge. He asked his assistant Rao about Qaf and Rao assured him that it would be located within a fortnight. Birbal fixed a meeting with Rao after a fortnight and in the meantime decided to seek ways and means to proceed to the Promised Land. His immediate priority was to obtain Mahaballi's approval. So without further loss of time he telephoned Mahaballi's office and sought an appointment, which was fixed. The earliest he could see Mahaballi was after six months. He felt happy. In Mahaballi's kitchen he had planted a junior cook who used to keep him informed about the dishes being prepared. One day, he rang up and among other things mentioned that the menu reserved for Gorby was being substituted by 16 menus. Birbal was intrigued. How come? he thought. He pursued the matter and contacted Goaty Gujral who had been India's ambassador to USSR. Gujral informed him about the disintegration of USSR.

"When did it happen?" Birbal asked.

"When! *Arey Baba*, it happened a year ago."

Bribal's whole plan to reach Kohi Qaf through Moscow was shattered. He could no longer obtain the 370 coins and 52 cards through KGB. He had to revise his entire strategy.

The tailor who stitched Mahaballi's clothes was a childhood friend of Birbal's. One day they crossed each other in the Chandni Chowk.

"Hello old pal, how are you?"Birbal asked. The tailor invited him to hot and sizzling Kababs at Karim's. Both sat in a corner and talked of their old friends. The tailor after a while jumped up and said, "Oh my god, I am late. I just forgot I have urgent work."

"What is it old man? Sit a while."

"No, no, Mahaballi's clothes are not ready and tomorrow he goes to Azerbaijan."

What? Birbal was aghast! Lady Luck, it seems, had decided to smile upon him. Now only if he could find a place in Mahaballi's entourage! Rao had told him that Kohi Qaf is in Azerbaijan. He left the tailor standing there and ran to Mahaballi's office. He had to move fast.

On arrival at the office he talked to his old friend Chander, the gatekeeper whom he had installed recently. He went with him to the visitors' lounge and asked for help. Chander was in a fix. How could he help his friend? Then an idea struck him and telling Birbal to wait for him he went inside. As it was late in the evening the babus had gone home; there seemed to be no one around. After some time Chander came holding a file and put it on the table in front of Birbal. They opened it and leafing through it came to a sheet of paper where they stopped. Here it was, the list of those accompanying Mahaballi. Birbal brought out his pen and added his name. It was so simple and easy that both laughed. The gatekeeper picked up the file to replace it in the office and Birbal took leave, as he had to prepare for his journey.

❖❖❖

After Jaladbhava's departure, Kashyap was left alone in the room. He began analyzing the events of the day. So Jaladbhava, it turned out, was not a demon after all and his men were also made of flesh and bones. Then why had they been presented as demons? Why had they been denied a good reputation? After all, they were highly developed and civilized people. He thought they did not kill me or harm me. They could have done anything if they wished. The king was so kind as to visit me. No, there is something that does not meet the eye. All ancient texts cannot be so wrong. The Guru's word cannot be wrong but what I saw with my own eyes could also not be wrong. If Jaladbhava was a demon king, then why did he not eat me and do away with me once and for all? Why did they allow me to descend into the valley, all the time monitoring my every move? Yes, Jaladbhava and his men appeared to be jealously guarding their territory. They held on to this Swarg Desh and this could be the reason for all outsiders to dub him and his people as demons, thereby justifying a holy war against them, seeking the help of Shiva and all other Gods. What should he do? Should he stay for a few weeks as permitted by Jaladbhava or should he devise a plan of wresting this land from Jaladbhava and his men and declare himself and his tribe as the eternal masters of this land. Kashyap continued to ponder over these questions. How could he conquer this land? A single unarmed Brahmin, alone and surrounded by thousands of Jaladbhava's men. It could be only through brains—*budhi*—and not through might—*Shakti.* He had to devise a plan. As he continued to delve deep into his thoughts, he was beginning to believe that he could take this country. Going back was out of the question. How could he give up this *Sunder Desh,* this *Swarg* on land? How? How? How?

❖❖❖

The ladies had started a big fire and were boiling water in earthen pots when boys carrying rice arrived. The hungry crowd mobbed the boys. Immediately rice was added to the boiling pots and the entire crowd waited for the meal. Maqbool Dar also arrived and, all the time looking at the hungry eager crowd, took his *hookah* and sat under a Deodar tree. From there he continued to watch these men, women and children as they waited for their share of boiled rice. Rice—rice was the only purpose, the only pursuit in their lives. What did they pray for, whenever they prayed, for yes, they did pray?

"Oh God, give us rice and then a long life."

Life was nothing without this magical yellow seed, which when husked yielded the snow white grain—the grain that sustained human life. Maqbool Dar continued to closely observe his own village folk getting excited and restive as the wait prolonged. The children began to argue as to who would eat more, men with pangs of hunger increasing rapidly in their stomachs shouted at their women, "Come on now, it must be ready, why is it taking so much time?" and women attending to the hearth waited with bated breath for the outcome of their toil.

Maqbool Dar called his friends Lassa Khan and Ajab Malik to his side. They talked in hushed tones. He told them that by the morning the State would come after them. Therefore, it would be wise to disappear during the night.

"Have your meal and go away."

"And what about you?"they asked.

"Do not bother. I shall also go, at the last moment."

As the men sat talking, the ladies brought down the mammoth pots from the hearths and the whole crowd gathered around them. No one was in a mood to allow the hot boiling rice to cool down; they just wanted it, whatever the price. The pangs of hunger rose to their heads, hot words were exchanged, fights broke out and slanging matches took place. Maqbool Dar knew that it would be impossible to control them. The commotion grew as the entire hungry crowd fell on the hot pots of rice and snatching, pushing and pulling each other, they began to eat. After the initial turbulence, things began to settle down and they ate without pausing for even a breath. They ate and ate.

Maqbool Dar watched in silence.

Rice rice come our way!
We will have you night and day
Cow too likes your golden hay
She then gives us milk &whey
Rice rice come our way.

A bright moon was shining on top of the forest and the crowd of men, women and children had, after years, eaten to their fill and now the entire crowd lay there asleep. Only Maqbool Dar was awake. He had not eaten a morsel. He continued to puff at his *hookah*. His friends Khan and Malik had departed and he was now considering the situation. Morning was round the corner. Another small stretch for the bright moon and then the sun would rise over the eastern mountains and the entire world would come to life. A new day would be born, but it would definitely be different from yesterday. Maqbool Dar was sure of that.

He stood up and went close to the sleeping crowd. Looking intently at each face he picked up the ten boys he wanted to talk to They were the boys who had transported the rice from the godown. He took them away from the sleeping crowd and under the Deodar tree he talked to them, "My dear boys, you are the only hope of this miserable nation. I do not want to lose you at this stage. By morning the troops will arrive and they will, as bloodhounds, tear at you all. So listen to me. Make good your escape through the woods. Scatter in the country and wait for my word. The day will come when I call you to rise in revolt and free your nation from the yoke. Till then my friends, God be with you. To you today do I pass on all my dreams, all my hopes."

With this farewell speech Maqbool Dar said good-bye to the group of youth who had taken part in the first act of defiance planned by him.

The convoy stopped outside Papa-2 interrogation center. Gani was brought down from the vehicle and in through a door, then pushed down a flight of stairs into a dingy room with no furniture in it. Two men in civilian clothes were already awaiting his arrival. He was made to squat on the bare concrete floor. Two chairs were brought in from an adjoining room and two men sat in them. One, an elderly man in his late fifties with a receding hairline, a potbelly and yellow teeth addressed him. "So you are here. We want to know certain things. If you cooperate with us, everything will be all right. No fear, but if you don't, then I can assure you of hell."

Gani just sat there on his haunches, his arms thrown around his knees, a vacant expression on his face.

"What is your name?"

The younger of the two interrogators began. Gani seemed to have completely missed that. The young man again repeated, "What is your name?"

Now Gani seemed to listen. He lifted his head and muttered, "Mulla Tahir Gani Kashmiri."

"What the hell? You are telling a lie. I told you this little room will turn into a hell for you if you tell lies." The man with the yellow teeth yelled. "Tell us your true name. We do not want any code names," the young man demanded.

"My only name is Mulla Tahir Gani Kashmiri—people simply call me Gani."

"He seems to be a hard nut, come we will have to be tough with him."Saying this, the pot bellied man got up and started for the door.He was followed by his companion, and Gani was left alone in that room.

After a brief interval, four men entered the room. The young man who had asked questions accompanied them. They carried thick ropes. Two men held Gani's hands and pulled them straight; two men held his feet and pulled his legs. He was suddenly lying prostrate on the floor. His hands were tied and so were his legs. Putting chairs one above another, a man managed to pass the end of a rope through an iron hook hanging from the ceiling. They fastened the rope to Gani's feet and with a sudden jerk pulled the free end of the rope that was dangling from the hook in the ceiling. In a flash Gani was hanging from the ceiling upside down. There he remained as the men secured the rope and left the room.

The only other person in the room was Gani's interrogator. He came close to Gani's head and pulling his hair thundered, "Thus hanging, you shall remain till the time you change your ways."

Saying this he tore Gani's shirt, throwing the shreds on the floor. Then he went up the chair and tore his pants and removed the shreds. There hung Gani, naked, without a soul near him, hidden from the world.

❖❖❖

The authorities considered it too risky to keep Yousuf Shah at Papa-2. They immediately flew him to Kot Balwal interrogation center at Jammu. There, he was treated well and provided a separate room all to himself. He was allowed to meet his friends who were already there. Even his relatives came from Srinagar to meet him. Yousuf Shah was really impressed with this treatment, although he would not forgive Birbal for the treachery.

Then one day all these niceties disappeared. On that day, the jailor brought over a top-secret confidential letter for him. It had come from Mahaballi's office. Yousuf Shah was thrilled to receive the envelope. With excitement and hope he tore it open and got out the beautifully decorated letter. He unfolded it and began reading the contents. It read:

To Yousuf Shah (abdicated ruler of Kashmir),from Mahaballi, the supreme Monarch of Monarchs. Be it known:

That, to break away the territories of Jammu and Kashmir from the kingdom you waged a war against the empire.

That you also conspired with foreign agents, through Nullah Khan and Ms RobinHood who have cast an evil eye on the paradise on earth.

That you did not arrange the wazwan for our Rattan Birbal at the appropriate time.

However, all these acts can be condoned if you agree and declare that the territory is an integral part, and you a humble subject of the kingdom, ready to join the national mainstream and you agree to the initiation of a political process in the valley.

If you agree to break away from all those who work against our interest, and, if you agree to the above, Mahaballi shall be pleased to appoint you as 'Naib-Tehsildar' of Tangdar.

Mahaballi

Yousuf Shah suddenly flew into a rage. He tore the royal letter into pieces and threw them at the jailor's face. This enraged the jailor who saw it as an insult to *Ain-e-Akbari* and bringing out the cordless phone from his shirt pocket straightaway dialed Mahaballi's private number. He informed Mahaballi of Yousuf Shah's behaviour and received fresh instructions.

Immediately, men ran into Yousuf Shah's room, removed his clothes and brought him out, and then paraded him naked through the jail premises and took him to the death cell. Here they chained him in a filthy dark cell. Two men entered and with iron bars beat his whole body blue and red. He bled from his multiple wounds. In the morning the floor of the cell appeared red and Yousuf Shah had passed out.

The sun's first rays cast a magical spell over the woods. Light pierced the dark canopy of the forest vegetation and reached the interior. Maqbool Dar sitting under the Deodar tree had gone into a slumber. The rays kissed his closed eyes and he woke up with a start. The entire village folk were fast asleep in front of him. They slept in gay abandon. Having had their full meal, they no longer seemed to bother. For a fraction of a second Maqbool Dar thought they were dead. Were they dead? How could they be dead? They had to be alive. He stood up, stretched his hands, looked around and saw a gushing stream a little distance away in a gorge. He set out towards the water. He would wash and pray to his God. The God in the heaven, for all the strength he would need. As he descended towards the stream, his eyes spotted a few riders down in the valley headed towards the stream, while a few others seemed to ride in his direction. He turned and went back to his sleeping comrades. He knew the state had moved, and he wanted to warn his fellow beings of the doom that loomed large in front of them. He called out to them. No one stirred. He shook them by their shoulders; he pushed them, pulled them, trying to break the deadly spell the sleep had cast. But he failed for not a soul stirred. He went back and took another look below at the riders. They seemed to be riding fast towards the woods. In a moment they would arrive. What should he do? Leaving the cluster of sleeping bodies, he moved away and, concealing himself behind a bush, began to wait.

As the riders finally negotiated the last steep stretch and came to the flat top, they saw the entire village folk lying there. They were soldiers of the Maharaja's force, accompanied by the Nambardar. The beast in them suddenly awoke, and quietly encircled the sleeping populace as they moved on their steeds. Maqbool Dar watched in horror as they brought out long leather whips. Then, acting in unison, they pulled the whips into the air and with a crash brought them down with the might of powerful state. As the leather caught the flesh of sleeping men, women and children, cries of pain, shrieks of horror suddenly broke out. Maqbool Dar watched as the soldiers lashed his men, women and children. With a vengeance, the soldiers hit, tearing and cutting the innocent flesh, and the mass of unfortunate humanity in horror and pain moved closer. So did the riders, hitting them hard. Maqbool Dar could see the leather lashes turning crimson red and shining as the rays of morning sun touched upon them. The soldiers continued with their task and then Maqbool Dar, unable to control himself any longer, picked up a boulder and took aim at the rider nearest to him. With all the might and pent-up centuries old anger, Maqbool Dar flung the boulder and it struck the rider's head. With a shriek he fell down and his horse sped away. The fallen soldier's companions rushed towards him. He was dead.

"Who did this? Who did this?" they asked and quietly Maqbool Dar came out of the bush, and head held high, shouted to them:"I did this, I did this, and I shall do it again and again. Till that day you leave us alone. I did this."

The soldiers pounced on him, brought him down and used all their lashes on him. When finally their anger subsided, they tied his hands and dragged him down the hillslopes. He was followed by the entire population of the village, who bled, moaned, cried, wept, from their own wounds but followed Maqbool Dar till they reached the nearest town.

❖❖❖

Lally Tigress was formally arrested at the airport and under heavy security driven to Papa-2. She was ushered into a small room where she had to spend her immediate future. Col Sharma accompanied her into the room and once they were seated began, "Look young lady, I will see to it that you are comfortable here. Of course, I will expect you to cooperate with the investigating officers. We would not like to use any 3rd degree methods on you but remember its use is not ruled out. It will totally depend on your cooperation. You may tell me if you need anything. Anything I can do for you. Personally I admire your courage. I wish it had been chanelled in the right direction."

Lally listened very patiently till Col Sharma concluded. Then very quietly she said, "Thank you Col. I want your help. I want my baby. I want to keep my baby here with me. I just can't keep it away."

"I can understand but it cannot be allowed I am afraid."

"Well then Col, my cooperation will depend on this alone. Get my baby and then send your investigators."

Col Sharma was dumbstruck. He knew nothing would change her resolve. If she decided to keep her mouth shut, no degree of torture would open it. He told her he would speak to his bosses and try his best. Saying this he took leave and went away.

Lally was now alone in the room. She examined the room in some detail. Strong sturdy walls of concrete with only a small window in one of the walls. The window was secured with heavy iron bars. There was a cot on one side and a chair lay on the other. That was all. An electric lamp scattering its yellow pale light hung from the ceiling.Lally sat on the cot. She was trying to understand how all this had happened. Who had given her away? No one except a few close associates knew of her movements. She had been in Delhi for the last three months and no one knew. She had gone there after her doctor told her that she was likely to have a complicated delivery. The doctor had suggested a hospital in Delhi and there she had been admitted a month before her expected delivery. She was treated well and gave birth to a baby boy who looked lovely with pink rosy cheeks. She had stayed there for two months after the delivery and then decided to fly back. She knew her organization needed her and she could not remain away for long. Even the girls who were very close to her did not know of her Delhi stay or of the birth of the baby. The security forces did not even know of her marriage.

Lally was sure of one thing—her captors would have to get her baby. She wanted the baby, and this was the only way to break the monotony and boredom of the prison cell. There were other reasons too. It would strike an emotional cord among her followers. The news that she was being held along with her infant in the prison cell would make a much better headline in the newspapers!

After an hour in the room Lally was beginning to get bored. What should she do? No one had turned up—no officers, no investigators. She understood this strategy. They were trying to break her by keeping her alone. Psychological warfare. She smiled to herself. She need not react. She must keep her calm. At that moment there was a sound outside her door. It opened and two men in uniform appeared. Lally was ready for the kill.

"You bloody dogs. Do you not know that even if you enter the room of your sister you must knock first and ask for permission to enter? Before I break your heads with my bare hands, you get lost."

The two men were taken aback; this was a real fighter. One of them managed to say, "You are our prisoner and you cannot dictate terms."

"Why can't I dictate terms? You bastard,do you talk like this to your sister or your mother? Has your mother not taught you this basic thing, that women, whether captive or free, are women and should be respected?"

The two men could not continue under this barrage; they just turned and closed the door behind them. Lally had begun to come into her own. The word quickly spread in the interrogation center that the lady had nerves of steel. For the next three days Col Sharma tried everything—cajoling, persuading, threatening but to no avail. On the 4th day he relented and informed Lally that her baby would be brought to her during the day but she could not keep it for more than a few hours. However, he promised that the baby would be with her everyday as long as she cooperated, and once the interrogation was over, she could have her baby permanently. To this she agreed and within a few hours her baby was brought and handed over to her. She held him close to her bosom and showered all her love on him. Even officers accompanying the baby could not resist shedding a tear or two in silence. When the officers had gone and closed the door behind them, she unbuttoned her shirt and putting her hand inside she brought out a breast and positioned the nipple at the infant's mouth. "Oh my darling baby, you must be hungry, feed on my love, suckle my milk—drink my blood for you are the hope—my future."

But the baby just shied away turning its little head sideways. The mother panicked.

"Come on my son, my darling my love have it, you must be hungry."

And with her free hand she turned the baby's head and again positioned his lips near her eager nipples. She could see drops of milk dribbling out but the baby looked uninterested.

"Come my son…come my Nund, do not shy away from me—I am your mother…come my shy little boy."

At this the baby opened its little mouth and grabbing her waiting nipple began to suck.

After two hours the officers appeared again and demanded the baby but Lally refused. She would not part with her baby. No law, no rule in any rule book could keep her away from her baby, whom she needed and who needed her. But the officers reminded her of the agreement and finally Lally had to give in. As the officers departed carrying the infant, Lally burst out sobbing. The steel in her appeared to melt away, and Col Sharma walked in escorting his ace interrogators. They thought this was the right time. She would break. But as soon as she saw the three of them she wiped her tears, willed the steel in her back, and flatly refused to answer any queries or to furnish any information regarding her outfit. Col Sharma sternly reminded her that as per the agreement the baby would be brought to her only in case she cooperated; to this Lally with a straight face declared that she no longer wanted the child. Col Sharma was totally flabbergasted. He had pinned all his hopes on the fact that Lally the mother could break Lally the tigress. He simply walked away from the room.

Later that evening the top brass analyzed the events and came to the conclusion that the baby still held the keys to Lally's locked mouth. But now it was resolved to use the baby in a different way.

Next day, Lally lying on her cot suddenly jumped up on hearing a baby cry. She reasoned that it was in the adjoining room and the baby continued to cry. Her intuition told her that it was her baby who was being tortured into crying in the next room. The persistent crying went on and on and finally Lally crossed the threshold of her patience. She began to sob, then she cried, she shouted, she shrieked; like a mad women she clawed at her face, beat her breast and tore her hair. She thumped at the wall, knocked her head against it, but nothing happened. The baby cried on.

After ages it suddenly stopped and Lally too became quiet.She lay there listless and still, fearing that any movement she made would again make her baby cry. Then quietly the door opened and in came the interrogators. One of them softly spoke to her. "We believe the lady wants to talk now." As soon as she heard him, she spun around rising up in a single move, her arms flung around him and her hands went for his throat. He was taken by surprise. His other companion tried to intervene. Lally gave him a kick in his groin.He doubled up with pain and Lally clawed at his throat. Some men immediately rushed in and went for her, separated the interrogator and brought her down. She continued to struggle and shout. "You inhuman beasts, how could you? How could you?" She became incoherent and inaudible. The gush of energy seemed to wane and suddenly the struggling and raging tigress became still.

❖❖❖

Ajab Malik and Lassa Khan walked slowly. After having taken leave of Maqbool Dar, they wanted to get as far away as possible from that spot in the woods before morning. They had started descending from the plateau on other side, avoiding the side on which their village lay. It was a full moon night and Lassa Khan was well versed with the area. For quite sometime they walked in total silence, perhaps going over the events of the last few hours in their minds. At last when they had reached smoother ground Lassa Khan broke the silence. "Now tell me where to go?"

"I do not know," was the short, matter-of-fact reply

from Ajab Malik.

"Okay, let me suggest something. Nearby lies a small village, Sharikpur. One of my aunts lives there. We can go there, spend a few days and wait for the news from the village and then plan our next move."

"Do you think Maqbool will give us away? After all we were in it." Ajab Malik enquired.

"No, I know him. He won't open his mouth, and moreover, it was basically his idea. We only collaborated."

"But we could have said no at any stage, we did not. So we are equally responsible. Look Lassa, I am beginning to feel guilty."

"Come on, how do you know that they will get Maqbool in the first place. May be he came out just after we left."

"No Lassa no, I know him. He will not leave his kith and kin to their mercy."

"Alright! We can talk about this later, for now just tell me, do we go to my aunts place?"

"Yes, as you think proper," replied Ajab. They began their journey towards Sharikpur. Lassa Khan by way of giving his friend more details began,"Look Ajab, you know why they call it Sharikpur? I will tell you. There is an interesting legend to this. It is said that in good old times one morning the Kashmiris woke up and were shocked to find that they had lost their tongue. Every one of them—each man, woman and child. None could speak a word. They had forgotten each alphabet, each syllable and each word. They could not communicate with each other. They suddenly turned into cattle or sheep. As the entire population woke up to this terrible happening, they came out of their homes and on to the streets. There was a huge procession. Everyone walked in silence, only sobbing with tears rolling down their cheeks, for dumb people can only weep and that too in silence. This huge procession walked towards the grand temple situated on a hillock. Once there the people sat and prostrated in the open courtyard of the temple. Their priests too had lost their tongue and led them in this silent prayer, weeping and sobbing. This went on for a long time and then you know what happened. A Sharika appeared in the blue sky. She flew down and over the crowd. Then she descended on to the vacant space in front of the prostrated crowd. On the ground she wrote with her fine beak all the lost letters of the alphabet they knew. As she engraved the first letter, people saw and remembered and spoke it aloud; then she wrote the second letter and people saw it, remembered and spoke it aloud; then she wrote the third letter; one by one all the letters were written by her, seen and recited by the people. And so in this way the people regained their tongue and they then named the script after the bird—Sharda. This little village where my aunt lives and where we now go is said to be that very place where the letters were engraved."

Ajab Malik seeing that his friend had concluded said

quietly, “Very interesting. That is a great tribute to Sharika.” The two friends continued to walk towards Sharikpur, whose insignificant hutments were beginning to appear in the distance.

❖❖❖

Raja Ram Dev and the two swamis were finally brought into a sleepy village situated in the foothills. It was surrounded on all sides by majestic chinar trees and had a fresh water spring, on one side of which stood the remnants of an ancient temple and on the other a beautiful little mosque. The three of them walked with cautious steps as being blindfolded they could not see. After walking for a while, their escorts ordered them through a door; they had probably come into a house as they could hear men and women talk around them. They heard the door being shut and then some one telling them to sit down. All three of them sat down on a straw mat. Then the voice again came.

“Remove their blinds, Let them see!”

Immediately their blinds were removed. Raja Ram Dev could slowly make out that he along with his companions was sitting in a dingy room, in what was probably a farmer’s hut. An earthenware lamp burnt in a corner and spread its yellow light in the room. He saw three men sitting in front of them, all carrying weapons in their laps. The one who appeared to be in command began without any ceremony.

"Now tell us who you are and what is your mission?"

"We are sadhus, we seek our lord. That my son is our only mission."

"Oh sadhu maharaj, cut it out. Tell us your name and your rank. Where is your HQ? I want to know everything and I will get it out of you."

"I told you my name. I told you who I am and I told you what I seek. Nothing more do I have to tell you son," Raja Ram Dev replied.

His interrogator felt uneasy. The man looked so calm and composed. There was not even a shade of fear on his face. He seemed to have a cool, calm and serene look. To hide his uneasiness and to reassure himself he fiddled with his gun and said, "Okay, what was your name before you became a sadhu? Your father must have given you a name. Tell me that name."

"Well, my name was Ram Dev," and pointing to the companion on his left continued, "He is Haruswamy." Then turning to the right said, "He is Maruswami."

With an expression of jubilation the man in front shouted out,

"That is Doraiswamy; what brings you back?You were let off once. Okay, very good. Now we can get some more of our Mujahids released."

Saying this he stood up and signaling to his comrades

walked out of the room. Raja Ram Dev looked towards his Gurus. They did not utter a word. A faint smile danced on Raja Ram Dev's lips, as he began preparations for his evening *samadhi*.

❖❖❖

Kashyap continued to roam the beautiful valley, realizing the Lord in His true colours. Splendid was his experience. Wandering through dense green woods, crossing silver brooks and emerald green meadows he was left in a state of total bliss. On one of his forays into the countryside one autumn morning he came across an expanse of water. The crystal clear water shone and radiated every ray of autumn sun into the surrounding mountains. It was breathtaking! A splendour he had never known! Kashyap settled himself on a rock overlooking the lake. Flocks of water birds danced around the lake. Kashyap thought of having a dip in this clear water. He somehow linked this dip to the ritual dip he used to have in order to wash away his sins on the way to Moksha. Well, he thought, having attained his Moksha, no sins clung to him. He smiled, got up and walked towards the edge of the lake. Removing his raiment he stepped into ice-cold water. A shiver ran through his body as the water touched his feet. He continued to walk. The water rose to his legs till he was waist deep in the lake. He began praying.

Uttering the holy words, he began lifting the water with his hands and wetting his body. The earlier shivers gave way to a feeling of cool comfort. He closed his eyes in deep meditation. Nothing appeared in the vast expanse of his thoughts. He continued to stand there, hands folded, lost within his own self, trying to seek the unknown, the unseen within his own inner being. Suddenly he sensed the water rising to his chest, then to his shoulders, and he opened his eyes. Everything looked the same, only he was descending. The ground under his feet was giving way and he was fast sliding in. Water continued to rise touching his chin. He tried to swim, splashing the placid water with his frenzied arms. It did not stop his slide. He was in great panic as water rose to his eyes and he could see nothing. His vision blurred and then darkened. He was falling into a deep black hole. Was this death?? This was Kashyap's last thought before he passed out.

❖❖❖

Ajab Malik was reciting his poem to a packed audience at SP College. A lean, thin, tall young man with intelligent eyes, dark, long and curly hair and a wide shining forehead, he reminded one of Shakespeare's Romeo. Girls idolized him. Boys either loved or hated him. He continued to recite verses in measured, well-articulated tones—a cultured voice, a dramatic delivery, right gestures with long tapering beautiful hands. Everything about this boy was right. He was earnest in his disposition, disarming his enemies with a smile, endearing his friends with a word. There in the audience sat Noshlab, a burqa clad college girl, sobbing at each verse delivered by Ajab Malik. Other girls were in raptures, clapping and conveying their feelings as loudly as possible. The college principal, Mr Kaul, a stern wise old man looked at the row of girls disapprovingly, but no one responded. Ajab Malik continued to deliver his entreaties to a stone-hearted damsel who did not reciprocate his love. That was the only thought matrix over which poets wove their poetic fabric. They sang to a damsel of unearthly beauty, who made the hearts of poets bleed through their eyes. But somehow, Ajab Malik, though conforming to the general trend of his age, appeared to be in the process of establishing a new distinct style. A new idiom seemed to be shaping up, for he not only sang of the damsel, he also challenged his foe for a dual. He presented the picture of a traditional Urdu Persian lover with a rose bud in his hand as an offering to his love, but one who also carried a sword to protect the rose.

Noshlab could not sob incessantly. She had to stop which she finally did. The Mushaira was over and people began to leave. Ajab Malik stood there responding to greetings of his audience, shaking hands and thanking all and sundry. A showman to the core, he was making the best use of a great performance. And then in the college lawn he came face to face with his damsel, Noshlab, the burqa clad daughter of a rich businessman of Srinagar. Her escorts were waiting for her at a distance and the decorated tonga was at hand. Ajab Malik did not utter a word. He dumbly stood there on the green turf waiting for Noshlab to speak. She did not say a thing. Ajab Malik waited.

She waited and ages passed between them.

❖❖❖

There was a feeble movement in her listless body securely tied to the cot on which it lay. A thick rope that was tied to the cot's posts tightly secured her wrists and ankles. Again her body stirred. Her breast heaved and her eyelids flickered. She opened her eyes. At first she saw nothing save a vast and deep darkness, a pounding in her temples. She closed her eyes. Now she began to think—yes she was alive and awake. In a split second her latest memories flooded her; the shrieking baby, the men in uniform and then the darkness. She again opened her eyes. She could make out the ceiling and then the electric bulb hanging from the center—yes she was in the same cell. Images began to clear. She wanted to turn her head; it ached; she wanted to lift her arm, it did not move. She sensed that her whole body was chained.

She moved her eyes to look at the surroundings. There she could see them—three shadows, faceless forms, black from head to toe, standing side by side. She concentrated her gaze on them. She could make out nothing except double rows of large white dazzling teeth. She felt scared. Who were they, these shadows with only a set of teeth to show. Ghosts, she thought, then dismissed the idea. She must be imagining things she reasoned and shifted her gaze back to the pale ceiling above her. But was she really chained to the iron cot? She again moved her eyes and with great effort lifted her head just a bit. Thunder struck her eyes. She was naked; there was not a stitch on her entire being. Her limbs securely tied she could not move. But her nakedness she could see. In shame she shut her eyes. Her heart began to pound at a ferocious pace. Sweat oozed out of her every pore. She could do nothing. She could think nothing. Her entire body suddenly became alive.

She felt as if her flesh was expanding in all directions. Naked, raw flesh. She clenched her fists. She tightened her being. She shut her eyes. And then it happened. She felt a claw descend on her big naked breast. She squirmed in disgust but did not dare to open her eyes. The claws dug deep into her breast. Nails sunk into her being. Then she felt thousands of claws all over her, tearing her, crushing her, tormenting her. She could take it no more. She had to do something. She tried to shriek but she could not.

Her vocal cords refused to move. She opened her eyes. She could see nothing. It was pitch dark and then in that dark tunnel she sensed those three pairs of white glistening moist dentures descend on her. It seemed an eternity passed. She lay there alive or dead, she did not know. She could only feel those claws, those jaws, tearing at her raw naked flesh and then suddenly it all came to an end. Jaws withdrew the claws withdrew. She opened her eyes. It was light all around. She lay there, utterly torn, bruised, and chewed. Her whole body was in a mess. She turned her head to locate those shadows. They were gone.

❖❖❖

Prime Minister Nozarkof had finally been persuaded to mention the Shimla mantra in the Joint Communique. Initially, Mahaballi had used all his wisdom but to no avail. Then finally the offer of an economic package worked. Of his own, Nozarkof wanted to talk of Islamic fundamentalism. Mahaballi was happy at that. No persuasion and no economic offers were needed. Mahaballi had a ready audience in Nozarkof after Nozarkof felt that Mahaballi's Din-i Ilahi could secure his throne against the neighbouring country, which was trying everything to destabilize his government. At the banquet speech, Nozarkof talked about apples, which his country could offer to Mahaballi's kingdom. There it was. Mahaballi's think-tank went deep into this issue. Did it mean Nozarkof knew of Kashmir's apples? The next few days were spent in ascertaining Nozarkof's real intention in offering apples. Mahaballi finally told him very bluntly that Kashmir's apples were an integral part of his kingdom and unless Nozarkof accepted this, no cultural agreement could be signed. Nozarkof withdrew his apple cart and had to accept the Shimla apples in return.

Birbal was having a nice time in the new republic. He toured extensively in the official car provided to him. He told his guide about the Qaf interest. His guide informed him that no one was allowed near the Qaf Mountain as nuclear installations of USSR days were located there. Birbal was in a fix. How to reach Qaf and lay his hands on the coins and the pack of cards that he had promised his friend back home. Finally he cajoled his guide to take him near the Qaf Mountain. He would only see it from a distance and return. They set out towards Qaf in the early hours of the morning. Passing through the beautiful countryside Birbal was reminded of Kashmir. The similarities were really striking, but he did not risk reporting this observation to Mahaballi, and even more importantly to Nozarkof and his men. Who knew how it may further complicate the matter?

By evening Birbal reached the place.

"There," his guide told him, pointing to a black mountain in the distance, "stands your Qaf, but as I have told you, you cannot go beyond this point." Birbal looked at the mountain. In the failing light it appeared more distant than it really was. Light reminded him of his lamppost friend. His heart ached for his friend, shivering in the open in freezing temperature at Srinagar. Remembering the plight of his friend and the promise he had made, Birbal resolved to reach the mountain and get the coins and the cards at any cost. For the present he told his friend of his wish to spend the night in the nearby hotel whose neon lights were twinkling in the background.

❖❖❖

Gani survived the forty days and forty nights of torture. He had withdrawn into himself, successfully shutting all doors and windows. Nothing reached him. All his wounds, the gashes, the cuts, the bruises did not pierce his self. He remained inaccessible and unattainable to his tormentors. They tried everything on his frail body but could not reach his spirit. In exasperation they gave up. They left him to die, the mangled mass of bones and torn flesh. His body lay there on the concrete floor of his cell. He was faraway, centuries away, ensconced in warm and cosy surroundings, watching the boat procession on the shimmering blue waters of Mar waterway. The officers of the camp decided to shift him to a prison. But could he travel? "No," the doctors declared. "Okay, sew him up, put him on his legs and then dispatch him to Tihar."

The doctors treated his wounds. His body responded and within a few weeks he was well. Then one day he was driven out in a vehicle and taken to a place a few kilometers away. There, ushered into the royal presence of Subedar Maharaj, he was made to sit on a plump sofa. The Subedar was announced, and entering, he took Gani's hand in his own. "Look my friend you are a genius. Mahaballi is a kind king. He wants you to visit the Royal Durbar. We shall arrange your journey. But let me tell you one more thing, good news, old chap. The political process has begun, and we want to start a new project, or rather, resume an old one. *Hawai Subh* is a daily newspaper printed on offset, glossy paper. We offer you its sub-editorship under an able journalist—yes, your namesake—you old chap you got me right. Then tell me, when will you travel and prostrate at Mahaballi's feet?"

Gani stood up and for the first time in centuries opened his mouth. "Tell your Mahaballi that Gani is mad."

"But how can I call you mad?" the Subedar enquired. To this Gani did not reply. He jumped onto the sofa, and then back to the floor, making wild gestures with his arms; with his hands he tore his own clothes, removed the turban and began chewing the cloth, all the time shouting, dancing, and jumping around the stunned Subedar Maharaj.

❖❖❖

Maqbool Dar was shifted to the central jail nestling among almond orchards. It was early spring and he could sense the fragrance of almond blossom in the air. The sun shone more frequently now but the cold breeze continued to bite. Maqbool Dar was the undertrial prisoner, confined to a small cell, but he was allowed a few hours outing in the attached yard. Once there, he would invariably think of his little village, the nondescript hutments surrounded by lofty mountains. The village with a pond of fresh cool water, the majestic chinar trees,the tall deodars and the pines. He felt lonely. He continued to compose his own songs and at times hum a tune. Sitting on a straw mat in the yard, he heard a strange sound. Someone was knocking at the nearby wall, which separated his yard from the adjoining one. He moved closer to the wall. He heard a voice, a hushed voice. He concentrated hard and gathered a few words.

"Escape plan is ready, wait for my call."

Who could this be? Who wanted him to escape from the prison? How could this be done? he wondered. He was, simply put, in a fix. He did not understand all this. But he had no choice but to wait. He could not do otherwise. That night he could not sleep. He continued to wait for some unknown caller who finally arrived. Maqbool Dar sensed a movement in the wall against which his head rested. He withdrew from the wall. Owing to the full moon peeping through the ventilator he could see a brick was slowly vibrating and then the vibrations became more intense. Before the brick fell to the ground with a thud, Maqbool had caught it with both his hands. He peeped through the gaping hole. He could see someone out there in the adjoining cell.

"Now let us make this hole wide enough for you to pass through. We have already broken open the outer wall. We are seven in all. Tonight, we shall be free; come hurry up."

Maqbool Dar did not know what he was doing but his hands moved frantically striving to remove the bricks around the gaping hole. One, two, three, four and the hole was wide enough for him to pass through. Maqbool squeezed himself out of his cell into the adjoining cell. Then his newfound friend unfolded the entire scheme in his ear. He would move out first, Maqbool would follow. Others who waited in their own cells would come one by one. They would all assemble under the almond trees and then plan the next move. Briefing him thus, he went down to cross the outer wall into which a hole had been dug. Maqbool followed him, step-by-step, cautious, never making a sound. He even avoided breathing for fear of being heard. His heart pounded louder and louder, till at last he fell on the soft, green grass outside the outer prison wall. His friend was already there, helping him to get on his feet. Maqbool felt free. He felt the fragrant cool breeze on his face, sweet moonlight engulfed his being and the soft green turf caressed his naked soles. Freedom! Ah! freedom, Maqbool thought.

Kalhan Pandit refused to move. The entire community migrated from his ancient village. Even his own children finally abandoned him. He ran after them. They refused to listen to him. His eldest son went so far as to suggest that the old man had gone crazy. Kalhan Pandit remained at Mattan, jealously guarding his heritage—the long and complicated rolls of genealogical tables. Each morning after his usual puja and a light breakfast, Kalhan would enter his late father's room, say his prayers in front of the neatly stacked manuscripts, wrap them in a sheet of cloth, tuck the bundle under his arm inside the long flowing pheran, and set out for the temple. A large pond surrounded the temple. Thousands of fish remained in continuous motion and pilgrims took it as a religious obligation to feed the fish; just watching the fish dance around was a joy. There each day Kalhan Pandit sat under the chinar tree that had been planted by his great grandfather. All his immediate ancestors had spent their lives on the same spot, updating their records, informing the pilgrims of their long forgotten ancestors. How could Kalhan leave this spot? Who would, in his absence, look after the records? Kalhan felt sad for his children. He had thought that his eldest son would one day take the records from him, but alas he belied all his hopes.

Squatting on the little wooden platform under the chinar tree, Kalhan looked around him. No pilgrims. No tourists. He was all alone in this sprawling complex. Was he right? For a fraction of a second he thought otherwise. He too should have gone. But then his resolve again overtook his weakness. He was right. He was right and time alone would prove it so. To divert his attention from his own thoughts he uncovered the bundle of records lying in front of him. Picking up a book he opened it and read aloud…

Rajiv Kumar Bhat S/o Dwarka Nath Bhat S/o Sat Lal Bhat

S/o Thakur Bhat

S/o Vasa Bhat

S/o Baib Bhat

S/o Suraj Bhat.

❖❖❖

Raja Ram Dev was squatting on the floor flanked by his two gurus. All three were captives in the hands of the gun wielding militants. They were lost in deep meditation. They did not recite any holy verses. They simply sat there with closed eyes and still bodies. Suddenly a little boy with his merry laughter broke their *tapasya*. All three opened their eyes and saw the little devil hiding behind the door. Raja Ram Dev called out. "Come here, come in." It took a lot of persuasion and cajoling to make friends with the boy. Finally he began opening up. There he sat in front of these old men, asking questions. And then with a dramatic air he announced. "I know you," pointing to Raja Ram Dev. "Do you?" asked Raja Ram Dev. "Who am I?"

"You are Bhishma Pitamah. I have seen you on television at my uncle's place in the city."

Raja Ram Dev laughed heartily. His two companions also joined him. The little boy was taken aback. He got up and left the room. Once their laughter ceased, Haruswmay, turning to Raja Ram Dev said, "Bhishma Pitamah Ji."

"Guru Maharaj, let us now think of the *Mahabharata* that is at hand. I have thought of a way to get out of this hole. Tonight we shall move but after putting all these people into a deep sleep."

"Here," he pointed towards a small pouch, "this *vibhuti* has to be added to the water pitcher before sunset. They will drink water with their dinner and they will go into a deep slumber. It will last for three days and three nights. Once they sleep, we make good our escape. Now who will put this *vibhuti* into the water."

They then discussed the plan in detail. At the appointed hour before sunset, Haruswamy would venture out and seek the kitchen. There he would move towards the water pitcher and if confronted by anyone plead thirst. Maruswamy was to have a dry run during the day to know the exact location of the pitcher in the kitchen.

Everything went as per the plan. They waited for a long time after dinner. When it seemed that all was quiet, Raja Ram Dev ventured out into the corridor, which on other nights used to be guarded by two young men. Yes, they were there but fast asleep, lying on the floor. He called his companions. Together, they inspected every room. Everyone was fast asleep. Raja Ram Dev beckoned to his friends to move out. As the three of them were crossing the outer threshold someone called, "Bhishma Pitamah." For a moment they froze but then slowly turned their heads. There in the doorway stood the little devil holding a gun in his tiny hands. "Take this with you and if some one stops you, shoot him down."

Having checked into the five-star hotel located just near the Qaf Mountains, which claimed to offer guests a splendid view, Birbal decided that the best way to pass time was to make the most of the situation. Russian vodka was his favourite. It somehow reminded him of the famous Patiala peg and he felt quite at home with it. Walking through the expanse of a wide lobby he entered the swimming pool area. There dozens of exotic beauties in swimsuits provided Birbal with a feast for his eyes. He sat unobtrusively in a corner holding his vodka and ogling at the beauties. He only missed his friend, who he imagined must be shivering out there in a dingy street in Srinagar. Anyway he was here only for him. He felt relieved. After a long time he got up and moved towards the restaurant. He wanted to eat. Sitting at a table he ordered his favourite dishes. As the well-mannered waiter laid the dishes before him, he noticed a troupe of Russian ballet get underway. It was a titillating show. Traditional Russian orthodox ballet had, after the freedom of Perestroika, evolved into a hybrid between ballet and cabaret. Birbal liked every bit of it. He again missed his friend. While he was staring at the ballet dancers, a sardarji came and occupied the chair at his table. He turned towards him. The sardarji began,"I just heard you were from India. I wanted to see you."

"Thank you sardarji," Birbal formally replied.

"Thank you. I own this hotel. You are my personal guest.

But let me introduce myself. I am Ranjitov Sin. I actually come from a little village Kala Bakra near Ludhiana. Now tell me about yourself."

"I am Birbal, I have come with Mahaballi on an official trip."

"Oh, you are Birbal. Oh good, very good. I know all your jokes. But why have you come to this place?"

"Well, I just wanted to see it," Birbal replied curtly, wanting to get rid of him.

"Oh no, do not hide from me. If you are after girls then just tell me friend."

"I am not after girls sardarji, I am after Qaf."

"Oh, Qaf?"

"Oh yes, state mission."

"Tell me sir, I, a true patriot, am at your service," beamed the sardar. Somehow Birbal was encouraged to share his secret with this man. Anyhow he may be of some help so he told him of his mission reinforcing the national importance of his work.

Sardarji was silent for a while and then he jumped up with joy. "*Twada kam hogaya samjo.* Only one person in the whole world and your good luck is that he is here now in this very hotel."

"Who is he?" asked Birbal in all seriousness.

"Guru Maharaj Swami ji. He is a great guru, a truly spiritual man. I will take you to him."

"I will be really thankful to you sardar ji if he is of any help."

"*Thank you wank you chado tusi saday Birbal ho ji.*"

❖❖❖

Though quite comfortably placed in the new surroundings Kashyap was not happy. He longed for the paradise he had lost. He wanted to roam in the streets of his own city where he had spent his days and nights befor emigration. He yearned to smell the long forgotten scent of almond and cherry blossom in the wind. He missed those chinar trees, singing brooks, and lofty mountains. He felt his strength and stamina failing with age. Could he ever go back to his wonderland? Would his rendevouz with exile never come to an end? He had no reply to these questions.

Then one evening, lost in deep thought, an idea struck him. He had now become an expert broker, but these small deals somehow did not satisfy him, though they provided him with enough to live a comfortable life. He wanted to do something big, to plan a great venture and to execute a memorable project. He had been thinking all through the night, while his wife slept comfortably next to him. As the morning approached and few rays of sunlight pierced the window, his mind received fresh enlightenment. The idea was simply great, out of this world. It would not

to the same jail. On his arrival at the prison, Charles received him with open arms. After all Yousuf Shah was a celebrity and every one knew of him. He had appeared on a number of international TV networks, and the front pages of major newspapers. Charles was impressed by his looks, the deep resonant voice and burning eyes. Yousuf Shah had also read about Charles in newspaper reports. Both were eager to know each other and in course of time they came closer. Charles introduced Yousuf Shah to Budshah. They somehow did not like each other but did not exhibit any animosity either. All three spent most of their time together, playing cards, chess, carom, or just gossiping about national and international affairs.

❖❖❖

Lassa Khan, the Superintendent of Police, surveyed the deployment of his force around the house. He was satisfied. A posse of policemen stood with him. One of his assistants handed him the megaphone and positioning it near his mouth, Lassa Khan blared out, "Maqbool, you are encircled on all sides. Escape is impossible. I command you to surrender, I will give you only up to ten seconds and if you do not respond, your hideout will be destroyed...ten… nine…eight. Lassa Khan continued the count down… even…six…five…four…. A window opened on the first

floor and Maqbool appeared. Lassa Khan stopped counting. His hand went to his revolver and he took position behind his jeep. Maqbool did not carry any weapon. He looked calm and at peace. He strode up the last three stairs and straightway walked to the gallows. He stood there like a rock. His head appeared to rise above the plank of wood that held the noose. He surveyed the scene in front of him: his own people, indifferent, lost in the mirth, merrily enjoying an outing in the Mughal gardens, partaking of a sumptuous wazwan. He called out to them but his voice could not rise above the popular film number blaring out and pervading the environment. He stood there in silence, watching beyond the horizon. The executioner approached him, tied his hands behind his back and lowered the sack on to his face. Charles Chopra was distributing sweets among the jail mates. After all, the country had been saved. The jailor congratulated Charles. Charles put a large *burfi* piece into his mouth.

That night, flanked by Budshah and Yousuf, Charles walked out of the prison gates to a waiting car.

❖❖❖

Kashyap opened his eyes to a dazzling light. Not able to bear the glare he closed his eyes again. Turning over the latest memories in his mind he felt he was dead and facing

Ajab Malik was strolling on the bund along with two of his close friends. They were his college mates. All three shared a common interest in Urdu poetry. Ajab Malik was particularly fond of walking over the dry crisp chinar leaves strewn all over the place. He remarked to his friends, "Do you hear the music these dry leave produce?" Majid reacted to this and said, "Melody is neither in leaves nor in your shoes; it is in your mind." Ajab Malik felt flattered for a while and this was an invitation to a long monologue on melody and the mind.

Som broke the chain of Ajab Malik's articulation and suggested that they all go to the Qalandar's Takia. This they had decided during the day. They came away from the Bund and straightaway headed towards the Takia situated a few furlongs away on an island inside the lake. Reaching the boulevard road they engaged a shikara and set out towards the tiny island. The evening was setting in and as they alighted from the shikara onto the shore, a thundering voice called the believers to evening prayers. Asking the nearest person about the location, they proceeded towards the Takia. It was a small place, just a room attached to a little mosque. As they removed their shoes at the door, a man appeared from inside and enquired,"What do you want?" Ajab Malik replied in a polite tone,"Sir, we seek the Qalander."

"Please, come on in," they were told. They went in. Ajab

Malik saw a score of men mostly past their prime squatting in a circle on the Persian rug covering the floor. The room was filled with smoke and the heavy sweet and pungent smell of hashish hung in the air. A man of considerable age detached from the rest sat near a window. A beautifully decorated *hookah* stood in front of him and he drew puffs of smoke from it. Ajab Malik and his friends walked the few paces and joined the men sitting in the circle. As they sat the man drawing at the *hookah* noticed them. Removing his hand from the hookah he murmured as if to himself, "Knowledge, knowledge...where is knowledge? This is not a college...or is it? Well it may be! Then I am the professor. Yes I am the professor.Come on children I will give you a lesson. He doubts me (pointing his finger at Ajab Malik) but they do not (pointing at Ajab Malik's friends). Now who is right? He or them? Both are right. Doubt is doubt. The doubter and the one who does not doubt, both are in fact right. Then both can be wrong. Wrong is wrong. Right is right. No wrong is right and right is wrong. The world goes on. But where is the world? I am the world. You are the world. I am dead. You are dead. The world is dead. But the world is the world and the world is alive. You are alive. Come near me my son." He called out to Ajab Malik, who got up and sat with the Qalander. His two companions watched the proceedings in awe. The Qalander broke the silence. "What do you seek my son?"

invited Ajab Malik to her apartment. This was her way of conveying her approval of her pupil's progress. Ajab Malik dressed in his Sunday best reported at the apartment. Miss Braun was waiting for his arrival. She looked quite different. She seemed to have spent sometime on her hair, face and the selection of her dress. He was stunned. Oh God! She looked gorgeous.

Teasing her, he enquired, "Hello, glamorous lady! Where is Miss Braun?"

"You naughty boy! Come in," was the friendly response thrown back at him.

Miss Braun led him into the living room. They sat side by side. She enquired, "A drink would be alright?"

"I am at the disposal of my hostess," Ajab Malik declared with a sparkle in his eyes. She got up and returned with a bottle of wine. Putting two goblets on the table, she opened the bottle and filled the goblets. Picking up one she handed it to Ajab Malik. Then lifting the other, she raised it up and brought it near his goblet.

"Let us drink to German language," she said with merry laughter.

❖❖❖

Guru Swamy was a big man. Long black curly hair dropping down to his shoulders provided the necessary

halo for the godman. A prominent big nose, two small slit like eyes and a long beard completed the facial detail. He wore a saffron coloured robe and strings of beads of varying sizes and shapes hung down his neck on to his chest. Birbal recognized him the moment he was ushered into his room by Ranjitov Sin. "Hello Guru Maharaj. Recognise me? I am Birbal, the same good old Birbal."

"Yes, yes! How are you Birbal and what brings you here?" Guru Swamy rose from his seat to take Birbal's hand into his own and led him to a seat by his side. Once settled the three men began conversing, discussing the weather and exchanging pleasantries. By and by, they came to serious business. Ranjivtov Sin introduced the subject of discussion. Guru listened patiently. Birbal conveyed all the details. "Well I can help you in reaching the caves of Qaf. But let me be very straight, no confusion old buddy. What do I get in return?"

Birbal thought for a moment. What could he offer? Perhaps the new locomotive deal or may be the defense modernization? Before he could come to a conclusion, Guru came out openly, "Look Birbal, the treasure you are after is worth billions. Wait a bit. You said 370 coins. Right? Do you know the price of each coin at, say Sothebys? It will not be less than ten million pounds. I will put the entire lot at around 3.7 billion pounds. I do not care about the cards. You can have them all. But I get half of the coins."

in a short while emerges a ray of hope for our nation to redeem its pride. We propose to utilize the services of this man in vanquishing Jaladbhava and taking his kingdom for all times to come." Nilnag stopped his little speech. Taking a cue, all the courtiers clapped their hands. A man rose and raised a flag shouting slogans.

Nilnag Ki Jai Pataal Ki Jai Jaladbhava Hai Hai Jaladbhava Hai Hai.

Presently order was restored in the court and Nilnag, taking charge again, commanded that the guest of honour be presented forthwith. In response, a string of fairies one after another flew into the court and descended onto the floor. One among them headed towards the king and began gyrating her body and swinging her wings. All other fairies taking cue repeated the ritual. The fairy then prostrated in front of the king. Other fairies followed. After a long pause the fairy lifted her head and rose to her feet. All others followed her. Then the king addressed the fairy: "Yes, produce the guest of honour."

"Yes my lord," the fairy replied and put her right hand into her left armpit under the huge white wing. She brought out her hand and placed a little diamond in front of the king. Positioning the sparkling diamond in the open space before the king she moved three steps away. Bowing her head, she joined her hands together and murmured a mantra. The diamond shook and then a cloud of smoke

rose from it and began dispersing into the air. As the smoke cleared everyone saw that a handsome man, elegantly dressed, stood with folded hands in front of the king, who said to him, "Kashyap, we welcome you to our court. We hope your stay has been comfortable." Kashyap bowed in gratitude and thanked the king for the hospitality that had been extended to him. The king then offered him a seat. Once seated in front of the king, Kashyap again thanked him. The king then began, "Our intelligence reported to us that a Brahmin of great lineage had successfully pierced the defences of Jaladbhava and was roaming in Kashmir without any hindrance. We followed this lead and came to know through our agents that Jaladbhava had taken kindly to you. We thought that we have a real opening in you. We, as a matter of fact, are not interested in the territory. We are a peaceful nation. We strongly believe in non-interference in other's affairs, but how can we allow an inferior race to be in command. This goes against our own basic doctrines of statecraft. Therefore, we have tried to modify the existing situation, but unfortunately we have not succeeded much. We also know of your desire to liberate the area. We will do everything in our power to help you in your noble mission. Believe us, it is our earnest desire to see you on the throne of Kashmir."

Kashyap considered each word spoken by Nilnag. Here was an opportunity of a lifetime! But how far would Nilnag go? Would he really help him? And if yes, then how? Could he not later on betray him? Kashyap was lost in his own calculations. Nilnag seemed to read his mind for he spoke very openly indeed. "Look my friend, rest assured that we will lay no claim to the territory. We will only see you installed on the throne. You will have complete freedom to decide your own future. We want no forced marriages, no imposed unions. You may do whatever you want, once order is restored. We shall never, I repeat, never come in your way."

That settled all the doubts that Kashyap may have had on the subject. He gave his word to Nilnag. Both got up and embraced each other, then sat down and resumed their discussions.

Nilnag's plan was very simple, and once accomplished guaranteed success. He would give Kashyap a magical *vibhuti,* a powder prepared by Nilnag over a period of one hundred years. Kashyap was to go back to Kashmir and invite Jaladbhava and all his ministers, nobles, commanders and all who mattered, to a dinner. During the course of the dinner Kashyap would serve the *vibhuti* in cooked fish, which Jaladbhava and his tribe relished. The *vibhuti* would put them to sleep. "How long would they sleep?" Kashyap enquired.

"That my son, I do not know, but it could be 40, 400, or 4,000 years. Once the *vibhuti* has its effect and they go into a deep slumber, all my fairies will descend and carry the sleeping men into a cave in the dense forest within the mountains. There they will be interred and shall remain. You will take the throne and the rest of the populace will obey your command. By and by, you ferry your tribe to fill the vacuum at the top and rule the land as you wish."

Kashyap was satisfied. After all he had to do as little as feeding the *vibhuti* and there was a strong chance that his life's dream was about to materialize.

❖❖❖

After a day's squatting near the fishpond under the chinar tree, Kalhan Pandit, carrying his burden of genealogical tables, headed home. Home, he thought as he leisurely walked in the street. What home? His entire family had deserted him. He was now all alone like a ghost, in his own big mansion. By and by he came into his own street and saw a hustle and bustle near his house—some people were moving in and others were coming out. A few trucks stationed nearby also came in view. Perhaps his children had returned. The thought flashed through Kalhan Pandit's mind. He prayed it were so. He almost ran the rest of the distance to his home. Crossing the outer gate he entered his courtyard. There he saw a young lady looking at him inquisitively. Kalhan Pandit moved near and said, "I did not recognize you daughter."

"Neither did I," said the lady with a frown.

"Well I am Kalhan Pandit. What do you want?"

"Nothing, what do you want? If you have to meet AC Sahib, he is not home."

"AC sahib? Whose house is this my dear daughter?"

"It is ours. Don't you know? The DC Sahib has allotted it to us."

"DC sahib? Well. It is fine. I am happy. After all this big house was almost empty and you can stay here as long as you wish."

"Pandit ji, what are you talking about? It seems you do not know my Sahib—the AC sahib."

"No daughter, I am afraid I do not know the present AC Sahib."

"What present AC? He was AC from the beginning of the movement and you say you don't know him."

"My misfortunate lady, in fact, I do not have much liaison with officers—now take your Assistant Commissioner..." The lady broke into laughter. "You simpleton, AC is Area Commander not Assistant Commissioner."

"Oh, yes yes I am hung in the past and what is DC dear?"

"It is District Commander. I told you DC sahib allotted this house to us. You know we have put our two children in the English medium School. It was getting difficult to send them to the town every morning though we have purchased a new Maruti car but you know life in a village is no life so we decided to move and here we are."

"That is a very good decision. Do you know my sons also moved away from here for the education of their children? Anyway can I go upstairs?"

"You know the boys have been clearing the place. I do not know. I am waiting for the AC sahib."

That evening Kalhan Pandit moved out of his ancestral house and into the small ramshackle room behind the temple, which used to be the grain store in the not very distant past. He carried nothing except his heritage—the long tortuous tables initiated by his long lost ancestors.

❖❖❖

Following Col Tarkunde of the medical corps at Cantonment Hospital Badami Bagh, Col Sharma entered the doctor's chamber. Col Tarkunde, the surgeon, offered him a seat in front of his small table. Col Sharma thanked him and sat down. The surgeon remained standing. Pacing the room, he was in a pensive mood. Both men kept silent for a while. Then Sharma broke the silence. "Well Col how is she now?"

"She will survive; you say she was mauled by a tiger. Well that would account for the multiple wounds, gashes, contusions all over her body, but how do you account for the devastation she seems to have undergone inside of her?" Col Sharma could not bear the piercing gaze of his friend. He turned his head sideways, without uttering a word. Col Tarkunde brought out a cigarette packet from his table drawer, and taking out a cigarette offered the pack to his visitor. Col Sharma nodded a no thank you. Col Tarkunde, lighting his cigarette and drawing a deep puff, again stared into Col Sharma's face and letting out a cloud of smoke said, "When shall we learn to respect human beings Col? It has taken me three hours to stitch her inside."

Col Sharma could take it no more. He exploded, "Come on man. She was not in the charge of the army. It is those bastards. What can I do? They are a law unto themselves." Col Tarkunde sensing that his friend had nothing more to say enquired, "Who controls them?"

"None," was the brief reply from Sharma. Col Tarkunde was taken aback. "What do you say? After all there is a joint command. Every force is subservient to this command. Why don't you do something about it? Read the foreign newspapers. Look what the world is telling about us." He realized that he was talking too much. He cut himself short and said, "Alright, I hope she will come out of anaesthesia in a couple of hours. But it is going to take a long time for her to get back on her feet."

Col Sharma stood up, picked up his cap from the table

and, offering his hand to Col Tarkunde said, "Please take care Doctor. She deserves it." Saying this he turned and taking big strides left the room.

❖❖❖

They had a sumptuous dinner—fried chicken with plenty of salad. Ajab Malik ate like a starved man. They did not talk much. After dinner his hostess proposed a cup of coffee. Ajab Malik volunteered to prepare it. Miss Braun was delighted. As Ajab Malik got busy in the kitchen, Miss Braun moved out into the balcony. It was a beautiful night; a full moon hung over the horizon. The dazzling city lights appeared to dim the soft silvery moonlight. Miss Braun sat on the steps and waited for him. She had been thinking deeply about this man. She thought him irresistible. There was something in this man—Miss Braun was unable to name it—something very tender, something very fresh and very gentle.What was it? She continued to ponder. Then in a flash she located it. It was something in his eyes. Sadness? Miss Braun questioned herself. No. Passion? No, then what? Love? Love? "Yes, yes, yes," Miss Braun said aloud. Ajab Malik, standing in the doorway holding two coffee mugs in his outstretched hands, heard Miss Braun saying, "yes, yes, yes." He simply said, "Miss Braun that is better—yes...an affirmation speaks of a positive bent of mind." Miss

Braun stood up, and taking her coffee thanked Ajab Malik, ignoring his remark. Both sat on the steps sipping their coffee. After a while, Ajab, unable to bear the silence that grew around them said, "How is the coffee?"

"Marvellous," replied the lady.

Looking at the full moon he remarked, "You know Miss Braun, this full moon always reminds me of a small sleepy village nestled in the dense woods of Kashmir."

"Any special event of your life?" enquired Miss Braun.

'Well, you know Kashmir is a beautiful place. May be I am biased, but I tell you Miss Braun it is splendid." Miss Braun was looking very intently into his eyes. Even in the dim light she could make out the flicker in his eyes as he cleverly sidelined the discussion from his person to Kashmir. She asked very bluntly, "Ajab, tell me who was she?"

"What do you mean Miss Braun?"

"I mean what I mean, you know what I mean. I have read a lot about the oriental mind. I know how it works. Love! Well it is not same in the occident and orient. Hell of a difference. I know now what keeps you ahead of all others. This vitality, this energy, this freshness, Ajab tell me about her."

Ajab Malik looked at her for a while and then suddenly dropped his armour. He was totally exposed now. In measured tones he began, "Well, yes you are right. She was a part of me as we grew up together. We came from different backgrounds. As two little children we played together. She was the daughter of a small time businessman. I come from a family of scholars, an elite family, a family respected for its ideals, for its scholarship and hold over letters. We went to school, and slowly came of age. Side by side, her father prospered. He became very rich. By the time we moved to college, the distance between our households had widened. Then suddenly it all came out in the open. We were desperate. My family disapproved, her father opposed. There was no way. It was doomed." Ajab Malik paused for breath and Miss Braun could see his misty eyes and flushed face. Putting down the coffee mug on the floor she touched his shoulder. He looked so innocent, yet so hurt. He resumed, "Well then, one day, unable to bear the whispers, her father took her away. For days and weeks I looked at the window desperately trying to catch a glimpse of her lovely face. But she was not there. Where had she gone? No one seemed to know." Miss Braun moved closer to him. He seemed to be shaking from head to foot. She took his hand and touched his face in a gesture of sympathy. Ajab kissed her hand. Miss Braun felt deeply touched.

She enquired, "What happened to her? Where had she gone?" Ajab Malik spoke as if in a trance,"Well, after months, one day I went to that little village in the dense woods. There sitting by a fresh water spring, lost in the memories of my beloved, did I tell you her name? No, I did not—well Noshlab spoke to me. There she was, a beautiful bird perched on the branch of a nearby tree." Miss Braun was confused. "What do you mean Ajab? Birds do not speak, and where was Noshlab in all this?"

"Yes Miss Braun, I too was surprised. But my Noshlab told me the whole thing. Her father had been mad at her; he took her to a Baba who lived in the dense woods. Baba, you know? People who shun this world in search of the supernatural, some sort of holy men, endowed with superhuman powers. As Noshlab was presented to this man and her father narrated his woes, the Baba asked her to give up and surrender herself to the wishes of her father. She refused. Baba got angry and in a fit of anger, chanted a particular mantra, threw a pebble at her head and transformed her into an unusual bird."

"That is unbelievable? Ajab Malik do you really mean it?"

"Yes Miss Braun, I know it happened. Noshlab told me all this and she was in the form of that bird when I last saw her," he concluded.

"But Ajab how is it possible? It is like one of those fairy tales."

"I know no one will ever believe me. But this is a fact. It is incredible, yet it happened exactly this way." Miss Braun, not wishing to hurt him, merely said, "Ok, you believe in it. That is all right and that is enough. But what happened later. Where is Noshlab now?"

Ajab Malik's face lit up as he resumed his tale. "Well, I stayed on in the little village. Every morning we met. Noshlab told me that the charm thrown over her by the wicked Baba could be reversed but she could not let me know how. She only advised me to wait for a particular night when the planets in the sky go into a particular configuration. She alone would know and she used to keep awake the whole night, looking at the sky and waiting for the auspicious occasion."

"Did she succeed?"

"No she did not for she was not allowed to succeed. One day she had called me to the flower bedecked meadow. She had to give me some important news. When I reached the particular spot, I found that she was not there. In the distance I saw a vehicle going down into the valley. Many tourists visited the meadow in that part of the year. On top of the vehicle stood a birdcage and I could hear the shrieking and wailing Noshlab, even from that distance. I ran after the vehicle. It sped away at great speed. The man who drove saw me running after him. He took me for a local tourist guide. He yelled in German, "I have got the rare bird."

"Oh! my god," exclaimed Miss Braun. "You mean your

Noshlab was taken away by a German. You are here in search of her?"

"Yes Miss Braun, yes."

"Oh, my poor darling! You have suffered a lot." Saying this Miss Barun wrapped him in her arms and held him tightly to her bosom.

❖❖❖

Reclining in the easy chair in the royal suite as the state guest of this moderate Central Asian republic, Mahaballi was in a joyous mood. He stood up and rummaged through his belongings. Then he stopped as he picked up something and held it up. It was an audio cassette. Yes, this one was Subhalakshmi's recital. It was a treat, he thought. Then his eye caught another cassette—Lata Mangeshkar's old melodies. This too was a treat. He was in a fix, which one to listen to? After much pondering, he decided to listen to both alternately. He walked up to the music system placed in one of the corners of his room. He put Subhalakshmi into the deck. He pulled his chair closer to the deck and settled down in it. The carnatic music filled the room. The evergreen voice of Ms Subhalakshmi rose. Mahaballi went into a trance. It was bliss. He stood up and pushing a button ejected Subhalakshmi, and inserted Lata into the deck. The nightingale began to sing. It was splendid—pure sublime bliss.

He once again settled down in the chair and seemed to go into a trance. After a while Subhalakshmi resurfaced in his mind. He got up and repeated the exercise. This went on for a long time. Then unable to get up for the nth time, he stopped the deck. Silence. He began thinking, his mind jostling with the huge challenge of how to listen to both simultaneously. He began rummaging through his belongings till he found what he was looking for—a pair of headphones. He put Subhalakshmi into the deck, connected it to the headphone and inserted the plug into his left ear. Then he inserted Lata into another chamber of the deck, connected another headphone and placed its plug in his right ear. Then he pushed the two buttons. Yes! Mahaballi had hit upon a novel idea for national integration. He made a mental note of it. He would talk about this in the next integration council meeting. Wise man, he thought and congratulated himself. He continued to sit in the easy chair, listening to the two queens of Indian music. Then suddenly he was distracted. The cordless phone in his shirt pocket began to buzz. He brought it out, pushed the in button and took it near his ear. He could hear nothing. He realized his folly. Quickly he removed the earplug, and listened. "Hello Hello," came from the other end. Mahaballi replied in his majestic tone, "Yes, Mahaballi speaking."

"Sir, it is Secret agent Raw Kaw. It is urgent."

"Yes, go on Kaw, what is it?"

"Sir, Birbal."

"What about him?"

"Sir, he has accomplished his mission."

"What mission? Give me the details."

"Sir, he has managed to enter the Qaf caves."

"Qaf caves. But why?"

"Sir, he is in search of the 370 coins and 52 cards."

"What? Did he lay his hands on the treasure?"

"Yes Sir."

"Oh! What a great betrayal! I will appoint a commission of enquiry. CBI will conduct a probe. But before that I will throw him out of the house and banish him to the forest."

"Sir, any instructions?"

"Yes, Raw Kaw. Find out where he is. And what is he up to? Keep me informed of every little detail. This is a national emergency."

"Yes Sir," said the agent and disconnected the line. Mahaballi's left ear became silent and he concentrated on his right. Ever melodious Lata was singing, *"Daga Nahin Dena, Zamana Kharab Hai Daga Nahin Dena...."*

❖❖❖

Kashyap was busy making arrangements for the grand feast. He had long sessions with the royal cooks of Jaladbhava's palace. He made detailed lists of different dishes that the cooks could prepare and which guests would relish. Fresh river water fish was ordered and different vegetables arranged. The cooks told him of the spices that they required and Kashyap took no chances. He wanted this feast to be a memorable one. He personally went to invite Jaladbhava, who at first showed some reluctance. After all, Kashyap was a guest of the kingdom and it was not proper for him to take the trouble. But Kashyap persuaded him and Jaladbhava agreed to be the guest of honour. Next, Kashyap contacted the chieftains and nobles of the kingdom and invited them to the great feast. Everyone was pleased with him. On the appointed day the sprawling lawns of the king's palace were illuminated and bedecked with flowers. Exquisite multi-coloured floorings were spread all over the place. The royal musicians were in attendance and seats for the king and his nobles installed. It was a full moon night; a cool breeze blew from one end carrying with it the fragrance of jasmine and roses. A little away from the site, hidden behind the bushes was the cooking space where scores of cooks dressed in spotless white aprons cooked delicacies on burning logs.

Kashyap inspected the area and enquired about the progress. The chief cook told him that everything would be ready by the appointed hour. Kashyap returned to the lawns and attended to the last details. As he was enquiring about the drinks, the first guest arrived. Kashyap received the nobles and escorted them to their seats. The royal band began to play. The stream of guests continued to arrive and Kashyap was soon fully immersed in the fulfillment of the duties of a good host. The guests dressed in their best, women bedecked in jewellary and fine raiments were a sight to behold.When the majority of guests had arrived, Kashyap ordered the drinks, which were served in beautiful painted terracotta goblets. As a full moon shone on the distant horizon, the king was announced. He had driven up in a carriage pulled by eight well-groomed steeds and Kashyap went forward to receive the royal guests. He opened the door of the royal carriage and a smiling Jaladbhava and his queen alighted from the coach. Kashyap bowed in great supplication. The king held his hand and the queen flashed a smile at him. Kashyap ushered the royal visitors and escorted them to their seats. All the assembly of men and women stood up and bowed as their beloved king and queen passed by. Kashyap remained in attendance. He personally carried the goblets of wine to the royal couple. The king thanked him and conveyed his appreciation of the arrangements made. After a while the feast was served and the entire congregation began to eat the painstakingly prepared food. Kashyap remained busy moving from one row to another, enquiring after his guests, ensuring that they were all enjoying the meal. When the feast was halfway through, he quietly withdrew and headed towards the cooking enclosure. The dishes yet to be served were lined up. An attendant guarded the urns and vessels. Kashyap asked him to fetch the chief cook. As soon as the guard disappeared from his sight, he quickly brought out the *vibhuti* hidden in his belt and threw it into the steaming fish. Just as he had finished mixing the magical powder, the chief cook arrived.

Kashyap gave him some instructions to change the arrangement of courses to be served and returned to wait on the king.

Around midnight droves and droves of Nilnag's fairies landed on the sprawling lawns of the king's palace. In a meticulously arranged operation, they flew away with the last sleeping man and woman. Kashyap stood there watching the horizon as swarms of fairies disappeared into the woods carrying the intoxicated flaccid bodies of Jaladbhava, his chieftains and nobles, ladies and gentlemen.

❖❖❖

Charles Chopra drove at a breakneck speed. Behind the wheel, his genius surfaced. His reflexes were razor sharp. After a while they approached old Delhi. Yousuf remarked, "Charles slow down now. You cannot maintain that speed in the busy bazaars of old Delhi." Charles smiled at him and taking a sharp curve said, "I can very well continue at the same speed but that will attract attention, so I will slow down." He applied the breaks, and went dead on the accelerator. The car steadied and began to run lazily. Budshah remained silent, watching the outside landscape in a detached fashion. At last Charles pulled into a dingy street and locating a vacant patch at the end of the street, headed for it, parked his car and all three of them alighted. Charles led the other two into a nondescript restaurant. Once inside, a strong smell of hashish hit their senses. It was a dark place and about a dozen men could be seen sitting in rickety chairs—some smoked charas while others drank. Charles made a brief visual survey of the place and straightaway headed towards the counter.

An elderly fat and bald man with yellow teeth and a heavy moustache sat behind the counter. Charles, resting his elbow on the counter, whispered something into his ear. The man jumped up in his seat and coming around the counter shook hands with Charles. Then he led the three of them through a side door into the interior cabin. As they sat around a small table, their escort picked up a phone, dialed a number and spoke into the mouthpiece in a low tone. Then replacing the receiver he turned towards his guests and said, "Sir, he will be here in five minutes; would you like a drink or is there any other thing I can do?"

"No thank you," said Charles,"we will wait for him."

Exactly after five minutes the door opened and a well-dressed gentleman in a grey business shirt, dazzling blue necktie, entered the room. Charles hugged him and listened to his report. He brought out a manila envelope. Charles took the envelope and opening it brought out a sheaf of papers. For the first time, addressing his companions, Charles said, "Look, here are your passports and air tickets. Your plane leaves from IGI airport after another 90 minutes. It will take you to Karachi and from there you are on your own." Handing over the documents to the two men, he looked quizzically towards the man in the blue necktie. Responding, the man brought out a few bundles of currency notes. Charles picked out a bundle and handed it over to Yousuf and said, "Now do not waste time. Take a taxi and straightaway drive to the airport. I will contact you later. Good luck friends."

Budshah spoke for the first time and touching Charle's arms said, "Charles, what about you? You are not travelling with us? Why?"

"Come on I've got a lot to do. I've got to settle some old accounts. It will take me some time and once free I too will fly."

Budshah could see the mist in Charles's eyes. He felt sad for his friend. In a sudden burst of emotion, Budshah stood up and hugged him. Charles was not ready for this.

Both looked at each other for a long time. Then Charles taking control of his emotions said, "Come on now, get going." Yousuf stood up and the two shook hands with their benefactor and friend and reluctantly left the room.

❖❖❖

Gani was returned to the interrogation centre. He continued to behave like a mad man. He jumped, shouted, shrieked, laughed, cried all to the utter discomfort of his escorts. Once inside his cell he tore at his own clothes. He went on shouting, singing, reciting his Persian verses and making faces at the guards, wildly gesturing with his hands. This continued throughout the night.

The commanding officer, a stern Sardarji, was informed in the morning. He called a meeting of his senior staff officers. There they discussed Gani. The police doctor was called and asked to examine him. During the day it was concluded that Gani had, in fact, turned insane and it was dangerous to keep him in. He was to be set free and shifted to the Mental Hospital. But the doctor cautioned the authorities that prior to shifting Gani they would have to drug him or else things would be unmanageable. At the appointed hour ten soldiers were pushed into Gani's cell to overpower him so that the doctor administered an injection into his wasted muscles.

Gani's body went limp as soon as the needle was withdrawn. Thereafter it was easy. Two men picked him up and laid him on the stretcher and placed it inside a vehicle. Within a moment the vehicle was speeding towards the Mental Hospital situated at the foot of Hariparbat hillock and surrounded by dense almond orchards. As the vehicle came to a halt outside the hospital building, Gani came alive. As his stretcher was being carried to the hospital building, he opened his eyes and stole a glance. The dense almond trees were in full bloom and Gani smelt their fragrance and a naughty smiled danced on his lips.

❖❖❖

Raja Ram Dev, accompanied by his two gurus, Haruswamy and Maruswamy, ran away from that little hut which had held them captive for four days and four nights. They ran one after another, Raja leading the way over the boulders, thorny bushes and steep terrain. It was a full moon night and they could see things very clearly as they tried to negotiate the hurdles in their way. All three men were gasping for breath but still they continued to run, their beards, their long hair and flowing robes, flying in the cool breeze. After an eternity they reached a plain patch of ground. There they stopped. A gushing stream was flowing nearby. They sat at its bank and quenched their thirst. At last the Raja spoke, "From here, you can see that mountain over there. There in the woods lies our cave. It is a steep rise from here on. But we shall make it before dawn. So come on, move."

They stood up and began the uphill trek. They were more confident now. Raja seemed to know the way. By dawn they reached the place and locating the crevice crawled in. Once inside the spacious cave, they stood up and feeling safe and secure abandoned all caution. They strolled through the cave. The first rays of the sun pierced the dark hollowness of the cave and they moved on. It was a never-ending cave, so it seemed. Tired from the travails of their flight, their legs sagged and they sat down. Raja Ram Dev saw his two companions stretching their bodies on the floor. He too stretched his limbs and all three of them descended into deep sleep.

Raja Ram Dev was in the dense woods, in hot pursuit of a deer. He heard the roar of a lion and smiled to himself. Big game. He moved in the direction of the sound, alert and ready for the kill and then it came. From behind the bushes leapt a lion straight at him. He grappled with the lion who went for his throat. The Raja caught hold of his paws. The lion attacked him with his teeth but the Raja held him back. The lion tossed him on to the floor. The Raja turned him over and went for his eyes. The lion managed to catch his throat and his sharp nails dug into his flesh. Raja opened his eyes. The place was teeming with men. A few of them were pulling him up on to his legs. Others were busy in getting his friends. Realizing that it was no dream, Raja stood up on wobbly feet and enquired from strangers,"Who are you? And what do you want?"

One of them, probably their chief, came forward and replied 'Jaladbhava Zindabad...Satisara Zindabad!"

"What does that mean my dear friend?" enquired Raja Ram Dev. The man in front replied, "The great monarch Jaladbhava is awake and Satisara is on fire."

Raja Ram Dev wanted to say something but his captors pushed him and his companions along the cave into the deep recesses and finally brought him in front of a throne on which sat a dignified man, attired in royal robes. Raja Ram Dev stood in front of him and a person rose from a seat in the rear and addressed the king,"Jaladbhava zindabad, Satisara zindabad. These three men, agents of Kashyap were found inside our outer caves. They have pierced our defence and are informers of our enemies."

Jaladbhava listened with attention and then enquired, "Who are you? And why are you here?" Raja Ram Dev took a step forward and without a bow addressed the king, "Salutes to the Monarch. We are no informers, Sir. We are men in search of God. Meditation is our creed. We were in search of a secluded spot to meditate in total peace. That brought us here. We are now at your mercy gracious king."

Jaladbhava, leaning forward on his throne, replied

to the entreaties of Ram Dev. "This is the same tone; we recognize it. Some 4,000 years ago, it cost us our throne—our kingdom, and our *Satisara*.We will not be fooled yet again men. Death upon you, for your death was ordained and forewritten by one of your breed thousands of years ago and now no treachery, no mischief shall prevail; our kingdom we shall regain. Our progeny, our own tribe shall retake what they had lost. We have arisen from deep slumber. The charm has outlived its use and we shall, yes we shall not rest in peace—death to you, all of you."

Jaladbhava rose from his throne and began to move. Raja Ram Dev realizing the situation prostrated in front of him.

'Mercy…king, mercy…king."

Jaladbhava walking away from him, murmured, "Mercy to the merciless shall not be granted."

❖❖❖

Guruswamy knew that Birbal would not keep his promise, yet he allowed him to enter Qaf and collect the treasure. Looking from the balcony of his hotel through binoculars, he saw Birbal coming out of the protected zone. But instead of heading towards Guruswamy's hotel he took the road to the city. This was enough for Guruswamy. Birbal's betrayal was confirmed. He picked up the cordless phone and dialed a number. "Hello, listen Raw Kaw. It is Swamy." Guruswamy gave the details to Raw Kaw, switched off the phone and sat down on the plump cushion. A mischievous smile danced on his thick dark lips. Stretching his bejeweled fingers he again picked up the phone, dialed a number and waited. Someone came on the line and Guruswamy began "Birbal is on his way to the States, I want him at any cost but alive. He carries a treasure on him. Save that for me. Is that clear?" After listening for a few moments Guruswamy said, "okay" and switched off.

There was a knock at the door. Guruswamy called out, "Come in". It was Ranjitov Sin, the hotelier. In his usual joyous mood Ranjitov came in and sitting in front of the Guru began, "Guruji I am beginning to get worried about Birbal ji. He has not turned up. Is he well?" Guruswamy cut him short with a wave of his hand. "Don't worry about him. He is already on his way to the States to sell the treasure."

"What? Has he contacted you Guru ji?" asked the startled sardar.

"No, he has betrayed me. I knew it too."

"Oh, my god! He betrayed you? He is such a scoundrel. *Tusi mainu daso ji. Main una noo sabak sikhawan?"* Ranjitov switched over to Punjabi. Guruswamy put him at ease. "Don't worry Ranjitov. We will take care of him."

As the two men were talking, Birbal was checking

into a hotel in the capital city. He was hungry and tired too. As he reported at the reception and asked for a room he was thinking of the ordeal ahead of him. He knew Guruswamy very well to let bygones be bygones. The receptionist handed over the key to him and an usher led him upstairs. Once behind the bolted doors Birbal emptied the contents of his pockets on the bed. Coins glittered in the dazzling lights of his hotel room. Birbal fondled these coins. "Beautiful," he thought. Then his attention shifted to the pack of cards. He sifted through the pack, shuffled it and studied it for a while. "Lovely," he said aloud. Leaving his treasure exposed on the bed, he removed his clothes and went to the bathroom. He wanted a bath. He completed his bath in record time. Dressed again, he placed the coins and the cards in his pockets and came out of the room. He headed for the lobby downstairs. He wanted to eat. Sitting alone at a table, he ordered his favourite dishes and waited. Looking around he spotted a gorgeous girl looking straight at him from her table. Birbal returned the glance. The girl gave him a dazzling smile. As the waiter laid the dishes in front of him, the girl rose from her seat and walked towards Birbal. The waiter left and the girl sat down at Birbal's table and asked coyly, "Do you need company, handsome man." Birbal was swept off his feet. He managed to exclaim, "Why not. Please join me."

The girl sat in front of him. Birbal invited her to dine

with him, which she accepted. Birbal continued to ogle at her from time to time. As they went through the dinner, he was sufficiently on fire. He invited the girl to his room and she gave him a hug. Hand in hand, they walked through the lobby, up the stairs and into Birbal's room.

❖❖❖

Lally tigress had gone mad. Her mind seemed to have shut down. She did not respond to anything. She seemed to see nothing, hear nothing and feel nothing. She sang incoherently whenever awake. Occasionally she went into total oblivion, but then came back suddenly singing at the top of her voice. The attendants who understood Kashmiri said her 'songs' were meaningless, incoherent and totally out of place. Her body however responded to the treatment. Her wounds healed fast and she could move about in the hospital ward unaided. The doctors seemed to be at a loss to know how to handle her. They called in a psychiatrist. He had a long session with Lally but failed to get a response from her. He concluded that the lady was in a deep shock and chances of her recovery were remote. Col Sharma continued to visit her. He felt sad for her. She did not recognize him either. She in fact recognized nothing around her. She did not care about anything. She seemed to have gone beyond everything. The top brass took stock of the situation. They studied the medical reports and discussed the matter with the psychiatrist. There was no hope. She was anyway useless. She could not give any information. So it was decided that she should be released and transferred to the hospital for psychiatric diseases.

She was shifted. She did not seem to register this change. The doctors at the hospital, all Kashmiris, were exceptionally nice to her. She had a reputation with the local people. They tried everything to restore her senses, but to no avail. She continued to remain far away—unattainable, unachievable, singing hymns to her soul. The hymns were incomprehensible to the ordinary mortals. She had, by and by, lost all sense of modesty. She would not mind being naked. In fact she would suddenly remove her garments and run wild in the hospital lawns singing and gesturing with her limbs. But in all such outbursts she was never violent. An attendant would calmly walk up to her and dress her up. She wouldn't object, continuing her singing.

On one such occasion, when she was basking in the sun, she had cast away her shirt and lay there on the green turf topless, with unkempt hair. She suddenly jumped up. Looking far away down the corridor she saw a few people leading a tall, turbaned man in her direction. She ran away in the opposite direction and into the doctor's room. The doctor was examining a patient at that time. Lally barged in highly agitated as if in pain. The doctor got up and came towards her. "Come on Lally. It's all right. Come on. What do you want? Come'. For the first time the doctor sensed that the lady was listening and would probably respond. Lally looked at him. Then covering her breasts with her hands she hung her head in shame.

❖❖❖

Yousuf Shah was a clever man. Charles Chopra had given him fifty thousand rupees to take care of the expenses. Yousuf did not want to share the money with Budshah. Otherwise also he did not have any special liking for his companion. As their plane landed at Karachi Airport, the two men came out of the aircraft and walked towards the airport teminal. Once inside, Yousuf Shah whispered something into Budshah's ear and taking long strides moved on. Budshah waited till Yousuf disappeared in the winding corridor. Then he resumed his walk. As he came out of the airport, he looked for his friend. He was nowhere to be seen. Budshah waited. Time ticked by. Passengers continued to arrive but Yousuf did not appear. Suddenly Budshah realized that he was all alone in an alien land and penniless. Where would he go? What would he do? As he sat there pondering over his miserable plight, a big explosion rocked the area. People began running helter skelter. Budshah also jumped to his feet and began to run. He did not know why he was running and where he was going.

He continued to run with the multitude of men and women on the street of Karachi. Barricades halted their march. Armored vehicles with soldiers in battle gear confronted them. Then all hell was let loose. Bullets flew in all directions and Budshah ran for cover. He ran into a nearby street. As he passed a wide open door, a fat lady caught hold of his arm and before he could respond dragged him into the courtyard. She shut the door and with a gurgling laugh said, "Do not worry. You are safe. You will enjoy. Come let us go in." Budshah did not understand a word. Why had the fat lady plucked him in? Why was she taking him into the house! Why were the people running? Why was he running? Who were the men in battle dress? Budshah was utterly confused. He looked towards the lady who beckoned him in. They went inside the house and into a spacious drawing room. He sat on a sofa. The lady realizing that the man must be tired went into an adjoining room and came back holding a bottle and a glass in her hands. She poured a drink and offered it to Budshah. Responding mechanically, Budshah held the drink in his hand. The lady said, "Come on take it man. It will calm your nerves. Then you can have a lot of fun." Badshah raised the glass to his lips and gulped it down, the liquid burning his throat.

❖❖❖

Ajab Malik roamed the streets of Berlin. Having completed his language course at Gottingam he joined the prestigious technical institute where he was supposed to learn the most up-to-date television technology. Walking through the streets of old Berlin was an experience in itself and Ajab Malik liked every bit of it. He did not know the place, so he began keeping a mental note of the turns he took and signposts he saw. After all, he had to return to his own apartment.

Germans, young and old, men and women crossed him as he walked leisurely down the narrow winding alleys, looking at the grandeur of old mansions, neat and clean surroundings. As he moved into a particular street it dawned on him that he was all alone. The streets were totally deserted. The windows of buildings lining the streets were tightly shut. He suddenly seemed to have entered a ghost town, a blind alley. He wanted to turn back but his inquisitiveness moved him on. At last he came face to face with it. The towering brick wall stood in front of him. Oh! So this is the wall, the Berlin Wall, dividing East and West. How odd and how silly, he thought. Man dividing the ground on which he stands, but what about the skies, the air, the fragrance of a flower, the flight of a bird. Ajab Malik did see birds flying across the wall, unmindful of the division.

Birds reminded him of his own bird.Where was

Noshlab? What had happened to her? What did that crazy German do to her? Oh God!' His own private grief overtook the concern for humanity and forgetting Berlin he turned and hurried back. By and by he came into a busy street. He saw people coming out of their homes to spend the evening outside. Some would just walk around; some frequented the well-kept parks but mostly people rushed to the pubs. Berlin was alive during the night. Neon lights sparkled everywhere. Ajab Malik had avoided being out at late hours. He would come out for a stroll after dinner and then hurry back to his apartment. He hadn't struck up any friendships so far and so had to spend most of his time all by himself. Walking back to his apartment, Ajab Malik was lost in his own thoughts. He had, for years, withstood the agony of separation from his beloved. But now in the lonely but beautiful and tranquil surroundings the pain became intolerable. If only once he could behold the beautiful face of Noshlab. Oh God! He would give away his life in exchange. But *kismet* or fate continued to deny him this. His search had finally brought him to Berlin. Would he ever find Noshlab? Would she really be around in some German town? Was that crazy German really a native of West Germany? Could not he belong to the East? Oh my god! What if he really belonged to the East? Ajab dismissed the idea, and then shook himself. Take charge, he admonished himself. Be calm, composed.

You need to have your thinking cap on now, push the emotions just a bit towards the back burner. He had to be from the West. But what could he do with the bird? He could be a scientist specializing in birds. Ornithologist? Or he could just be a bird collector. These Germans have funny hobbies. Some collect rags, some collect worn out shoes; could be that this particular German was just a bird collector. Collecting exotic beautiful birds, caring for and watching them suffer.

Lost in his usual agonizing thoughts, he came to the street that led to his apartment. Taking the last turn, he saw the door of a nearby pub open and there she was! Ajab Malik froze in disbelief. The blonde, beautiful girl wearing a sky blue top and a navy blue denim skirt came straight towards him. As she approached, she sensed that she was being keenly observed. She walked up the remaining steps and came face to face with Ajab Malik. He wanted to say something but no words came out of his mouth. The young girl stopped, smiled and with a giggle said, "Eh man. Want me?"

Ajab Malik managed to say "Hello my No...."

He could not complete 'Noshlab'. The girl took it as a 'No' and pleaded, "Come on man. I don't cost you much. Just a good dinner, some nice wine and a whole night, so cheap my man!" The words just floated in and out of his ears. He was unable to understand what the girl meant.

He just stood there like a zombie. The girl took his arm, and almost pulled him towards her.

❖❖❖

Kashyap was enthroned as the supreme monarch of the country. Nilnag himself attended the investiture ceremony among others. It was Nilnag, who, amidst the recitation of the sacred hymns and burning of incense, placed the crown on Kashyap's head. Nilnag's chieftains and nobles remained in attendance. Jaladbhava's populace watched the ceremony as mute spectators. They knew that they could do nothing; their leader had been removed from the scene. Jaladbhava's army had been disarmed and completely neutralized. Nilnag fulfilled his promise at the religious ceremony by placing the crown on Kashyap's head. He then proceeded to address the gathering. He said, "People of Kashmir, today is a great day in your lives. It is a great day in the life of your nation, so rejoice and be happy. For you have been delivered from the yoke. Demons have ruled you for long. Those who have been removed were truly Rakshasas and divine providence has intervened to bring them to their end. Kashyap is a noble of royal lineage. He is wise and learned in the matters of state and religion. Follow his word and you have nothing to fear. Disobey him and you shall perish."

Saying this Nilnag sat on his seat beside Kashyap. The majority of the audience remained silent. Only Nilnag's own men raised slogans and cheered their king. When silence was restored Kashyap stood up and addressed his new subjects. "When the world sleeps, Satisar wakes up to the new dawn. We will run the affairs of the state in accordance with the divine law. We thank Nilnag the great monarch for his guidance and help in freeing this nation from the clutches of the inferior race of the Rakshasas." Saying this, Kashyap sat down and a heavy silence fell over the place. No one raised any slogans, no one clapped and no one cheered.

At last Nilnag got up and so did Kashyap and the ceremony came to an end. The country had thus passed from the hands of Rakshasas to none other than the grandson of Brahma—Kashyap, and was to remain as such.

❖❖❖

Rachel turned out to be a terrific woman. Birbal had never imagined even in his dreams that a woman could be so insatiable. Since the moment the two entered Birbal's hotel room they embarked on a journey of wild lovemaking, which seemed to go on and on, exhausting Birbal totally. He had tried to match her passion and keep up the tempo till midnight but finally felt sapped of all energy. He dozed and fell into a deep slumber. Rachel kept on needling him for a long time but there was no response from Birbal's limp body. Once sure that the man had finally run out, Rachel sat up in the bed, stretched out her arms and stood up. Throwing a glance at the sleeping man, she turned over, stood up, and entered the bathroom. She knew she had all the time in the world. She leisurely got into the hot bathtub and submerged herself completely in the hot water. It felt good relaxing. She just lay there allowing herself to get over the recent exertion. At length she began scrubbing herself, rubbing every pore with the luxurious soapsuds. She felt on the top of the world.

She came out of the bathtub and put on the shower. Streams of warm water hit her body and the soapsuds began sliding down her glistening skin. Once clean, she walked out into the bedroom, water dripping down leaving a trail behind her as she walked on the plush carpet. In the center of the room she picked up a large towel and began rubbing herself dry. She threw a glance towards the sleeping Birbal and smiled. "Fool," she said aloud, and then throwing the towel away crossed the room to the closet where her clothes lay entangled with those of Birbal's. She carefully separated her clothes, putting them neatly on a chair nearby. Then she picked up Birbal's clothes, one by one, going through the pockets, emptying them, and laying the contents in a pile on the table. Throwing away the last bit of his clothing she looked at the assortment of articles recovered from his pockets. A pocket watch, passport, wallet, keys, a small pocket book, a few bills. That was all. She opened the wallet. It was bursting with currency notes. She threw it down in disbelief. She stood up and looking all over the room headed towards the small table at the head of the bed where he lay fast asleep. She opened the drawer. It was empty. She lifted the mattress corner—nothing there. Where the hell have you hidden it? she almost screamed in rage at the sleeping man. In the next hour or so she had searched every nook and comer of the room but the treasure she was after was nowhere to be found. She gave up in disgust. This nut was really hard. She resolved to crack it any way. She threw a glance at the sleeping man and moving towards the bed said, "I will find it, you bastard, even if you have hidden it in your bowels." Saying this she jumped into the bed and snuggled close to Birbal who seemed to respond to her frantic touch.

❖❖❖

Gani came really alive. The poet in him woke up from a deep slumber. The fragrance of almond blossoms knocked at his senses and transported him to another world. Not far from the mental asylum stood Fani's hermitage. A vast expanse of land at the foot of a bare hillock, studded with almond trees in full bloom. Dara Shikoh had set up a library of rare books and manuscripts for his philosopher and guide. There were living quarters for Fani, meditation cubicles for his disciples, a glorious mosque whose floors and walls and ceiling were studded with thousands of precious stones. Fani was in his own hermitage. Dressed in a flowing embroidered gown with a large round white turban on his head he addressed his pupils who squatted on a Persian carpet in front of him. In the front row sat his blue-eyed boy, Prince Dara, shorn of his royal attire, simply dressed as a seeker of truth. Gani sat with him and others sat behind them. Fani dwelt deep on his concepts of human brotherhood. He had completed work on his treatise on religions of the world. *Dastaan-e-Mazhab* was the point of discussion. He held that faith and religion were two different entities, one may supplement the other but the two never intermingle. Faith was simple and unitary in disposition. The ultimate being was supreme, omnipresent, all encompassing. This was faith and common to all people of the world. Religion, on the other hand, constituted a set of beliefs and practices which, depending on time and space, could differ amongst men. Faith on the other hand, was one indistinguishable quantity, undivided, whole. Faith could coexist with any religion, whereas religions couldn't and would clash one with the other. His book had set religious bigots on fire. This was total blasphemy. He was accused of being a heretic, and religious authority handed down *'Hukme Kufr'* on him. In all this Fani remained unmoved. He religiously defended his alleged irreligiosity and held his ground. Dara Shikoh, listening patiently to every word his guru spoke raised his hand. Fani noticed and fell silent for a while. Then looking at Dara with those piercing eyes enquired, "What is it Dara?" Dara sat straight and with a bow replied,"Great and wise teacher. I have a question."

"Yes, go on, ask."

Dara responded: "If faith is one, if God is one—if the entire mankind is one, why so many religions?" Fani smiled at his pupil, then casting a glance over the entire congregation began, "Dara has asked a fundamental question. If Faith is one, why religions are many? The moon shines on a moonlit night, if you look up at the star-studded sky, you will find millions of stars shining, sparkling. But then night gives way to a dawn, the sun rises in the horizon and the moon, the stars, they all become invisible. Faith, my dear Dara, is above the stars, above the sun and the moon. They shine at their own appointed hour, depending on time and space. They are all in harmony with each other. Imagine if they cross each other's paths what would happen? A catastrophe. All religions must travel in their own orbits and never, I repeat, never cross each other's path. This is the crux of my book. This is the crux of God's word."

Gani sat silent, imbibing Fani's every word. The

discussion shifted to Fani's latest 'fad' as his critics called it. The 'Kasb-e-Mah', or 'Taming the Moon'. Dara had got a sort of an observatory constructed halfway up the mountain overlooking not only the picturesque Dal Lake but almost the entire valley. On a full moon night Dara, along with Fani and a select few, performed a set of rituals directed at imbibing the luminescence of the moon. They believed that the moonlight not only invigorated the body but also soothed the soul. This practice had become a point of discussion among ulemas and Fani and his band of followers were ridiculed for adopting pagan ways.

At the end of the discourse Fani addressed Gani, whose latest composition he wanted to hear. Gani was reluctant to say anything, but Fani would not let him go. Gani finally read a few of his verses and Fani stood up and came to him. All those present got to their feet. Fani embraced Gani, kissed him and said, "Gani, from now on you are fit to be my tutor, this today I declare, though it was long ago that you had actually surpassed me in knowledge, intellect and wisdom."

❖❖❖

Kalhan Pandit, lying in his bed and unable to sleep was sure that he had heard a knock at the door. This room was where he had taken refuge after banishment from his palatial house. He sat up in bed and became all ears. Presently he heard it again, louder and persistent. He stood up, lighted a match and then a candle. Fearful and apprehensive he walked to his door. In a hushed tone he enquired, "Who is there?" A commanding voice responded, "Open the door." Kalhan unlatched the door and it swung open under pressure from outside. He moved aside and three young men wielding AK-47 rifles barged in. Kalhan Pandit was now totally terror stricken. He felt his end had arrived. His legs began to sag. His throat become dry and a cold shiver ran through his old frame. One among the intruders shouted at him, "Come pandit, you are wanted." Kalhan moved a step backwards and hit the wall. Weakly he managed to ask, "Where? Where am I wanted?" The youth gave him a taunting smile. "You will know, come let us go." His two companions held Kalhan by his arms and began moving out. Kalhan made on effort to pull himself together and managed to walk.

Out into the street a taxi had been parked. Its doors were thrown open and Kalhan was shoved into the rear seat. He was sandwiched between two men holding guns. The leader of the squad sat in front along with the driver. The car began to move and in a while came on to the main road. The leader of the party turned back, looked at the frightened Kalhan and reminded his boys that the prisoner had to be blindfolded. One of them caught Kalhan's collar and pulled up the pheran above his head. Kalhan tried to protest but could not. His head was now totally covered and the car continued to run on a deserted road. After what appeared to him as an eternity, the car came to a halt. He heard the doors being opened, the men got down and one of them pulled him and brought him out. He was led to an adjoining house. Once inside they entered a room on the ground floor and made him sit on a mat. He was ordered to wear his pheran properly and show his face. As he pulled down the pheran and opened his eyes he saw five of them squatting in front of him. The one seated in the middle reclined against plump cushions. He looked straight at Kalhan. It was a menacing stare. Kalhan shivered. Unable to bear the suspense any further, he began in utter desperation, "Son, why have you brought me here? What have I done? Please tell me."

He was about to break down. His tormentor perhaps sensed it.With a reassuring smile he began, "Panditji! you are an old man and we respect you. We have nothing against you so please be at ease. It is a small matter. We have been informed that you...well. Let me be very clear. One of our contacts has informed us that you maintain records of the Mujahideen, their whereabouts, activities and so on. We are inclined to suspect that you are working for RAW. So we thought it necessary to confront you. You see we cannot tolerate any informers amidst ourselves." Kalhan Pandit was really horrified. He knew that everybody who was killed was an alleged informer. He began to plead. "No, no! I am nobody's informer. By God I tell you I am not linked to anyone. I am a simple man, deserted by my own sons. An old man like me, what should I do such a thing for? Nono, someone has given you a wrong brief. Please believe my word. I do not maintain your records."

"Then what records do you maintain?"

"Oh! those records! These are ancient records, initiated by our ancestors. They are genealogical tables. The history of families of kings, nobles, men in high places."

"But we too are noble."

The interrogator picked a hole in Kalhan's submission.

"We aren't fit enough for your records?" Kalhan was at his wit's end.

"No sir, it is not like that—you see we only add to the existing tables."

The interrogator continued with a twinkle in his eyes, "Oh, and we do not exist in your tables. Why?" Kalhan could only manage a feeble reply. "Well what can I say."

He realized the futility of arguing a lost case. His interrogator gave a short laugh. "Pandit is cornered. But let us leave it at that. Tell me, all your sons have escaped from the valley." Kalhan saw a ray of hope; he could perhaps generate a bit of sympathy.

"Yes son, they have left me alone." His tormentor placed

a hand on his shoulder and said, "You have a lot of property. A big house, plenty of land. What do you propose to do with it?"

"What can I do?" Kalhan knew what was coming. The commander asked with a straight face, "Do you have any cash?" Kalhan stated honestly, "Only few hundred rupees."

"Oh no, I mean bank accounts etc."

"No my dear, I have nothing," was Kalhan's honest answer.

"Then Panditji, I am sorry but you are doomed," the young man said in all seriousness.

With a shiver running down his spine Kalhan muttered, "What have I done? For God's sake tell me."

But his interrogator had now assumed the role of the jury and he pronounced his verdict. "Your guilt is proved. Now you have an option—either you pay five lac rupees in hard cash or you die. Choice is yours."

Kalhan Pandit began to shiver. He pleaded with folded hands, "I have no money. How can I pay you such a big sum?" The man interrupted his pleadings, "You can, even if you have no money, you can."

Kalhan could not understand this. "How, how can I?"

"We will arrange the sale of your property; the money so realized will save your life. You have only to affix your signatures on some papers." Saying this, the commander looked towards one of his men who got up and left the room.

In a moment he returned accompanied by an elderly person holding a bunch of papers in his hands. He handed over the papers to the commander who placed them in front of Kalhan. The Commander rose from his seat and began to leave the room. At the door he turned back and said, "Pandit ji, I hope you still carry a pen. Boys look after him well—his son was a friend of mine." Saying this he moved out and closed the door behind him.

❖❖❖

Madam escorted Budshah into the hall. There stood a string of beauties in front of him. Pointing to the girls, she said to him, "They are all at your service, chose the one you like most. They are fresh and delicate like the Jasmine petals from the garden. Look at her, she is Mahjabeen, truly moon face, and look at the curves. She comes from Baluchistan. Here is Mahpara the beauty from the Frontier. Look at her eyes and the black hair. And lo! there is the beauty queen, Zoon, from Kashmir. Behold her red cheeks and black eyes. Choose Sir, choose, they don't cost you much. You know, before the turmoil in Karachi, they cost a fortune, but now, no customers. It is a job to keep this joint going. Near starvation we are, yes." The Madam continued drooping her jaws to convey a picture of misery and want. Budshah silently surveyed the grils. Suddenly the Muezzin's call to the believers from a nearby mosque rent the air. As a reflex, the madam stopped in mid-sentence and covered her head with the dupatta that hung from her shoulders. All the girls present there repeated the ritual. The Muezzin continued "*Allah-o-Akbar, Allah-o- Akbar*...Allah is great... Allah is great...."

When the Azaan concluded, the madam lifted her stretched hands to her face, closed her eyes, mumbled a short prayer and rubbed her face with her palms and straightaway resumed business. "So what have you thought? Which one would you take for the night?" Budshah, as if in a trance, managed only a few words, "Madam! This is sin."

"Oh come on Sir! What sin? We have complete arrangements here to avoid the sin, thanks to our brothers in Islam, I mean the Arabs. You chose the girl. I will call the moulvi who is on our payroll. He will perform your Nikah. You will take your wife, and in the morning you divorce her. Pay her Haq meher and of course a little bit of money for the room and services. It is so simple and in no way sinful."

Budshah could say nothing. It was really foolproof. He continued to stare at the girls standing in front of him. He did not know how to get out of it all, his own plight seemed so wretched to him. The Madam was beginning to get impatient with him and so were the girls. They had begun whispering among themselves and then there was a thud at the door. Without waiting for the response, the intruders barged in. They were ten in number and all were in uniform, the soldiers of the Islamic Republic. One of them, perhaps their senior caught hold of Madam's plaited hair. "You old bitch, what is going on here?" Madam had seen the likes of him before. Unruffled, she replied, "Come son, do not maltreat your mother." The man gave a twist to her hair. Madam writhed in pain but blurted out, "You dog what do you want?"

"Ah, that is better," said the soldier, "I am taking all your daughters' (pointing to the terrified girls), the sahibs have a party."

"Ok! Leave my hair. How much do you pay?"

"Not a penny, you old sow." He released her.

"That is unfair, soldiers are kind."

"Do not flatter me, you fatso. Just pack them in the vehicle and go to sleep." Then as if noticing Budshah for the first time he turned to him and said,"Go to sleep with your pimp."

The soldiers then caught hold of the girls; no one protested. They followed their captors as silent lambs. Madam continued to plead with them for the charges. As the party moved out, Budshah was left alone, standing there in the middle of the room. After a while the soldiers drew away carrying their birds of prey and madam returned to Budshah. As she came close to him, she unbuttoned her shirt and exposing her large fat breast and holding it out to him said, "Won't this fetch me even a simple meal?"

❖❖❖

They had a couple of drinks in the nearby pub. From there they walked hand in hand to Ajab Malik's apartment. Once inside, Ajab seated the girl in front of him and looking deep into her eyes began, "Look, I am Ajab Malik and you, you are my…"

"I am your girl friend for the night. My name is Angela. No complications. Is that clear?"

"I am your Ajab. We loved each other. We were separated. We lived in Kashmir."

The girl laughed. Ajab watched her, completely at a loss for words. At last she said, "Come on man. I never went out of Germany. I wanted to but no money to visit places. I was born here in Berlin. I don't know what you are talking about."

He tried for a long time to convince her that she was his long lost love. The girl listened to him patiently and at the end said, "Look here, either you are crazy or there was a girl out there at your place who resembled me. That is all. Come on. Don't spoil the fun. You are a stranger to this place. Get ready, I will take you to all the places." Ajab had to reconcile to the situation. He had intentionally kept out the bird story while pleading with the girl. But now alone in his bathroom where he had gone to change, he began to think. Could it be that the bird collector had set her free and she had somehow regained her human form but not her past, her memory? Ajab continued to think. His chain of thoughts was finally broken by Angela's knock at the bathroom door, "Come on man, do you intend to sleep there?" He came out and after a while both set out on their journey to Berlin's nightlife.

She was his guide and Ajab handed himself over to her. She decided that it was time for dinner. They entered a restaurant and she ordered for both of them. They hurried through the dinner and then left the place. Out in the open she said,"There is a place. It is called the Underground. We will now go there. You can enjoy yourself thoroughly. Everything is there. How about Hashish? Do you like it?" she enquired. Ajab Malik said nothing. They walked on and finally reached the place. It was really underground. They had to descend twenty-five to thirty steps and then move through a long winding subway, at the end of which stood the Underground World. There was practically everything there—hasish joint, drug parlours, bars, and of course the sex den. At the hashish joint they saw young and old Gemans smoking hashish from beautiful pipes. Some having oversmoked lay prostrate on the ground. Others stood quite calm while yet others talked incessantly among themselves. Angela could not resist the temptation to draw at the pipe. She freed her hand from Ajab Malik's and went for it. He tried to dissuade her but before he could do anything she was drawing frantically on the pipe that a young man held out to her. After a few puffs she slumped down into the lap of the young man.

Ajab watched in horror. An old German with a stoop materialized in front of him. "Son, take heed, the allies are coming. They are knocking at Berlin's doors. Where is the Fuerher? Do not worry the Fuerher is there. As long as he is there, glory is to the German Reich. We will overcome. Do not worry, do not worry." Ajab gave him a patient hearing. Suddenly, the German seemed in no mood to talk. He fell silent, closed his eyes and remained still. Ajab moved on. The rising smoke from all around got into his lungs. His eyes watered. His sight blurred and he was unable to see properly. He searched for Noshlab. Where was she? There were dozens of girls and boys lying on the ground, their bodies entwined, flesh intermingled. Who was Noshlab amongst them? How could he separate her from the heap even if he located her? A disgusted Ajab Malik moved on.

There were four chairs around a small table. Three men sat in them while one chair lay empty. The men looked very old, with shining long hair and beards. All three wore black robes. They seemed to be debating some important point. As Ajab appeared they saw him. They fell silent and one of them beckoned to him to take the empty chair. Ajab was mesmerized into acceptance. He moved to the chair and sat obediently awaiting the next command. The man who sat on his right patted his shoulder and said, "Young man! Ah young man! Youth, yes youth. Superman's youth is eternal. Yes. He will not age with time. He will emerge on the horizon and control the entire world." The man next to him intervened. Lifting his right hand and pointing directly at Ajab, he said, "This young man. Do you see this young man?" he enquired from the person on his left. He nodded his head. Then he asked the man sitting on his right. He too nodded his head. Then he gave a satirical laugh. "The young man who sits there and the young man you two see does not exist." Both the men turned to him in disbelief. The man continued, "Yes he does not exist because you do not exist. I do not exist. Existence is a mere doubt."

Ajab Malik was beginning to get frightened. He was probably in the company of men not quite in their right minds. He made a slight movement to get up. The gentlemen sitting on his left placed his hand on his thigh and said, "Rational theory demands that I ask you a set of questions. You will answer them; then I will analyze them. We may have to take help from a physicist, a chemist, a biologist, an anthropologist, a dentist, a psychoanalyst and so on and so forth." The other two gentlemen gave a measured laugh. The man looked at them with contempt and said, "You don't forget that the Feurher considers me as his teacher and out of your entire lot he only adores Clausewitz." The two gentlemen lowered their heads. He turned his attention to Ajab and said, "Are you ready? Who are you?"

"I am Ajab Malik."

"Which kingdom?"

"Kingdom? What do you mean?"

"Plant kingdom or the animal kingdom?"

"Oh! The animal kingdom."

"Order? Class? Species?"

The man was filling answers into a sheet of paper in front of him. When the questioning was complete, the gentleman studied the paper with great interest. He went on studying it. Then he got up and walked to a nearby cupboard, opened it and brought out old worn out books and placed them on the table. He sat down and went through the books, one by one, reading and throwing an occasional glance in Ajab Malik's direction. Then he closed his books, stood up and holding the paper in his hand said to Ajab, "I have identified your type but how do you surface here? You are already extinct." Ajab was startled. He got to his feet and was about to move when the old man said, "I sympathize with you, but your struggle for existence has ended; you were not the fittest, you go and enter a fossil and don't disturb anything."

Ajab Malik walked away from there. He was really sorry for having been there. It was a place for nuts, he thought as he came to the end of another corridor and moved into another chamber.

❖❖❖

However hard she tried she couldn't locate the treasure. In utter desperation, she decided to try the direct approach. Fondling Birbal's cheek she said, "I salute you, you are great."

"What do you mean?" asked Birbal.

"I mean what I mean, no hide and seek dear, you know I was after the treasure you stole from Qaf. But I couldn't locate it. You are a genius."

"Oh that…" Birbal felt flattered. "We are masters in the art of concealing things, my dear."

"Alright, now listen carefully. Yes, you have done it, but you cannot hold it. You know Raw Kaw is after you. Guruswamy has set his hounds in search of you. They won't let you have the treasure. But if you take my help you will succeed."

"How?" Birbal enquired.

"Look man, I should not be saying this but now there seems to be no other way. I represent the CIA. I offer you a deal. You pass on the treasure to us and in return we give you any number of dollars you demand and that too in Swiss banks."

"Why is the CIA interested in the treasure?"

"Don't ask me this. You can only satisfy yourself of my antecedents. Wait a bit." Saying this she got up and moved to the little table where her clothes lay. She picked up her denim jacket and bringing out her identity card returned to Birbal and handed it over to him. "That should settle it. Look, you have no choice. I guarantee your life and also your fortune."

Birbal held the card in his hands and began to think. He realized that the lady was right. Mahaballi and Guruswamy, both must be after him. He could take a chance with this girl. But somewhere an idea surfaced in his mind. He said, "Basically I was doing it for my friend who wants to win the jackpot at the casino in Delhi. What does he get in the event of my accepting your offer?"

"We will take care of him, okay."

"It is a deal."

They kissed each other. Then Rachel got up from where she sat on the bed and said, "Now get ready. We don't have much time. We have to get out of here. I will make a few phone calls and directly proceed to the airport. We are on our way to the States."

Birbal had no option now. He stood up and moved towards the bathroom. Rachel went to the heap of clothes and began to dress. Once through with it she came back to the bed and picked up the telephone. She gave an outer number and replacing the receiver waited. Presently there was a buzz. She lifted the receiver and told someone to make arrangements for her flight to the States. She heard the reply for a while and then thanking her contact severed the link and replaced the receiver. Birbal showered and came out of the bathroom fully dressed. Seeing him Rachel informed him that the flight was in two hours and it was important that they start for the airport immediately. He agreed and crossing the room went to the cupboard, opened it and brought out his suitcase. He stuffed his used clothes and others things into the case and closed it. "I am ready," he informed Rachel. She looked at him in a thoughtful way and said, "Where is the treasure? Birbal it is better if you give it to me here. You know, no one suspects me, so let me carry it."

Could he really trust her? He debated the question in his mind and after a while replied, "If the CIA was unable to find it, no one can. Let it remain where it is."

"Birbal, it is one thing to conceal something while you are stationary. It is something else when you move. Look, so far the treasure could have been concealed anywhere in this suite. Now it has to be either on your person or in your suitcase. That makes it very easy. Hope you see my point," Rachel explained patiently.

"I do see your point. But I assure you that even now the treasure is beyond anybody's reach. Why don't you try again?"

Rachel took it as an open challenge. Furious at him she took two steps towards him, then stopped and yelled, "Don't move. Remain where you are."

"Okay," he responded with a mocking smile.

He stood there and Rachel went through his pockets, felt every part of his dress, his body, then ordered him to step out of his shoes; she could not find the treasure on his person. "It has to be in the suitcase." She ordered Birbal to remain where he was and moved to the suitcase. Birbal flung the keys into her waiting hands. She opened the case and searched. She searched every nook and corner of the case. She went through every item in it. She did not find the treasure. Now she was totally disgusted. She sat there watching Birbal. "Unbelievable, incredible. Oh God!" She jumped to her feet. Have I been taken for a ride? The man probably has no treasure at all. But then my information could not be wrong, she thought to herself. She thought hard and was furious; she had to do something. She yelled at him, "You son of a bitch. You have no treasure with you. You have been simply deceiving me all this time and do you know the consequences?" Birbal simply smiled at her shrugging his shoulders. This put Rachel on fire.

She put her hand into the pocket of her jacket. It was a

reflex action but her revolver was gone. Birbal continued to stare at her. Very casually he moved over to the bed, lifted the corner of the mattress and brought out the revolver. As he turned, Rachel saw him standing in front of her with his hand drawn out and carrying her gun. She was totally crestfallen now. But Birbal came to her rescue. He flung the gun into her direction and said, "I don't think it is required where you can use your brains—come now it is getting late."

"No," Rachel, holding the gun in both hands, thundered, "You are not moving out from here unless you tell me where the treasure is." She advanced menacingly towards Birbal. But he stood his ground, never losing his calm. He quietly replied, "Cut it Rachel. Your revolver is empty. Again it is brains. But I shall tell you where the treasure lies."

She was totally flabbergasted now. Her hands fell down and she stood there utterly outwitted by this clever man. In total resignation she lifted her eyes to him and said, "I trust you completely. Now if you please, do tell me where it lies."

Birbal was flattered and quite excited. He began to dance around the astonished lady and sang as best as he could—*Choli Kay peechay Kya Hai? Choli Kay Peechay…* She said nothing, just watched him sing and dance around her. She understood no word of what he was singing. Then after a while he stopped and Rachel asked, "What was that?"

"Oh my God,you don't understand Hindi!"

"No, not a word," she replied.

"In that case I shall have to tell you that the 370 coins are glued to the inside of your *Choli*, that is your bra. I fixed them as you enjoyed your bath at night."

Rachel inadvertently put her hand inside her bra.

"Oh my God! You are right, but where are the cards?"

"Safely glued to the inside of your pants, my dear lollypop," said Birbal to the dazed CIA agent.

❖❖❖

The old mental hospital renamed "Hospital for Psychiatric Diseases" by a missionary who spent many years managing the patients there was on fire. The fire started in the rear of the sprawling complex and spread very fast. It was a holiday and most of the hospital staff were away. The few men on duty tried everything but could not prevent the fire from spreading and in a short while leaping flames engulfed the entire complex. People living nearby rushed to the spot. The fire brigade took its own time in reaching the place. Volunteers risked their lives and extricated the patients. Most of the inmates were just watching the flames disinterestedly. In all, 79 patients were rescued and moved to the nearby poultry farm. Late in the day the hospital superintendent and his staff arrived. They took stock of the situation. The entire building had been razed to the ground. The fire had been extinguished but a thick cloud of smoke continued to rise leisurely and spread in the sky above.

The doctors checked their patients, counted their heads. After a number of checks and cross checks they concluded that two patients were missing. A young doctor was quick to note that Lally and Gani were not present. The hospital staff was of the unanimous opinion that both of them had remained inside the burning hospital and had most likely been ravaged by the flames. What no one knew was that as the fire had begun spreading Gani had managed to enter the room where Lally had been sitting unconcerned with her head hidden between her knees. He had lifted her to her feet, dressed her in a pheran and moved her out through a back door. No one had seen them as they sped away from the burning complex. They straightaway moved towards the hillock, passing under almond trees. Gani continued to hold her hand as they walked. By and by they reached Fani's hermitage. Gani recognized the place even in its dilapidated condition. It was in ruins. Gone were the days when it would be teeming with students of Fani. Gani and Lally sat there in the courtyard of the once grand mosque. After a brief while, Gani stood up and leaving Lally there to rest for a while moved in. He wanted to see the place properly. Who knew Fani may be there, seated on his favourite couch looking straight above the Lake at his favourite spot—the lonely observatory on the mountains. Gani went into the mosque. No one had come to pray. Gani looked at the Imam's place where Fani would lead the prayers. From the mosque Gani moved to the adjoining ruins. Here were the cubicles for Fani's pupils. They were of course empty. In one of the cubicles a bitch had whelped. Her little pups were moving here and there, waiting for their mother to return. Did Fani know of this? Gani wondered and moved away. Lastly he reached the lion's den—Fani's own quarters where Gani had generally been a witness and sometimes a participant in the heated discussions. Here Fani would be at his argumentative and eloquent best.

Removing his shoes outside, as was the practice, Gani went in. The room was empty. Gani walked cautiously towards the exalted place where his master used to sit. He was apprehensive. He expected Fani to materialize from the void and in his unique style admonish him for being late for his discourse. But nothing of the sort happened of course. He sat down and closed his eyes. For a long while he sat there, motionless, lost in the recesses of his own being. He thought of nothing and then it came. He felt a hand descend on his shoulder. He opened his eyes. He turned his head. The hand moved away from his shoulder. Gani began to stand up. "Keep sitting," Fani commanded.

"Master where are you?" Gani spoke in anguish. Fani's familiar laughter filled the room. "It is pitch dark. Master give me light," Gani prayed.

"You...yourself, you are the light, the cause and the effect of light. Why do you demand light, Gani?" Fani lectured.

"Master I am lost in time." Gani began but Fani cut him short.

"Time is one single entity. How do you divide it to know you are lost? If you are lost, you are lost from a place, then you are present at a place, and from whence did you fall prey to such vile thoughts?"

"Master I do not know," Gani submitted.

"Yes that is it. You know that you do not know. That is the ultimate of knowledge. Perfect and complete knowledge. Rest of it is all trash."

"Master tell me, this upheaval, turbulent Dal, what is it?" Gani asked.

"You are talking of the rocking boat, the strong wind and the dark sky? The boatman, gone to sleep, discarding his ores? Don't worry. The cloud will pass. He will arise and steady the boat," Fani said, and his words, magically, seemed to fill the room with light. Gani got to his feet. He looked around him. No one was there. He shouted at the top of his voice; "Master, Master." But there was no reply. He came out of Fani's enclosure and headed for the mosque. He had begun to worry about his companion. He entered the courtyard. Lally was gone.

❖❖❖

Like a wounded tigress madam paced the floor of her drawing room. She had been on her feet the entire night. Budshah lay slumped on a sofa. It had been a terrible night for him too. Suddenly a loud voice rose from the nearby mosque and shattered the still atmosphere of the last remnants of the night. "*Allah-o-Akbar, Allah-o-Akbar*". As a reflex, madam stopped pacing the floor. She lifted her hands and covered her hair with the dupatta that lay across her shoulders. Budshah opened his eyes but did not move. The Azaan was delivered. The morning had arrived and with it came the rumblings of an approaching automobile. It seemed to become louder and louder till finally a screeching sound announced the arrival of a wagon. Madam ran to the window. Budshah got up from his seat and followed. A wagon was stationed outside. The chauffeur came down, and moving around the automobile came to the opposite side and opened the door. Many voices emanated from inside the vehicle. The driver held the door open. One by one the girls alighted. Madam was overjoyed. She turned to Budshah, "The girls are back. Praise be to Allah." Budshah could clearly see a tear roll out from her eyes. She turned her head to look again. Budshah also concentrated on the scene outside. The girls came out and then a tall bearded man alighted from the vehicle. The driver bowed in reverence.

The man wore a long flowing gown. His head was covered with a huge turban. He appeared to be around forty years of age. The long black beard shone in the early morning light. As he became visible, madam blurted out, "Here comes the vulture." Saying this she moved away from the window and waited in the center of the room. Budshah continued to stand near the window. The door was thrown open and the girls trouped in. One by one they came to madam. She hugged them all. Not a word was exchanged. At last madam said in a low voice, "Girls, you must be tired, go and catch some sleep." The girls marched away in silence and disappeared into an adjoining room. As the girls departed madam saw the turbaned man enter. She remained where she was looking straight towards him. He strode in with big majestic strides. As they came face to face, he raised his right hand to his forehead and addressed her. "Now tell me, am I not a sincere man? Your girls... well, I have brought them back to you. I have told you a number of times but you do not listen."

"Thank you for the trouble," was what madam could manage.

"No trouble my dear. It is my duty. I take the opportunity to renew my offer. Money is no problem. You quote the price. I want this place. You can stay on. Your girls can stay on. I only want to launch a big company. It will be known as Tourism Promotion Corporation of Pakistan (TPCP). You see there is a tremendous market. Our Arab friends, rich friends will be our clients. This place will be the HQ. Tourists will arrive here and from here they will be allotted the companions—your girls, and of course many more girls who are waiting to be rescued from the dirty hands of kufar behind the LOC. These tourists will then travel to tourist resorts that we will construct. Come on lady.Wake up to a new dawn. With God's grace it will be a great venture."

Madam spoke briefly and to the point,"But Maulana, what do I get in addition to the price for the dwelling."

"Yes, that is better. Whatever you want. After all, you have the required experience. We value that. How about a partnership? Say ten per cent. Believe me, you will roll in millions and it will be absolutely safe. No hassles with police or the rangers."

"But I know them, they won't let you go without their pound of flesh," madam interjected. The man gave a short laugh. "Oh yes, but I have taken care of that. We have two ten per cent chunks reserved for the right persons. With God's grace, the foundation stone will be laid by Bibi herself."

"You are a bastard," madam opened up at last. The man just laughed at that. "Then it is a deal."

"I think it is ok." Madam smiled, apparently pleased with the deal just struck. The man turned around and for the first time spotted Budshah standing there with his back to the wall. He seemed to lose his cool. He almost yelled at his newfound partner, "Who the hell is he and what is he doing here?"

Madam looked towards Budshah and then towards the man. "Oh him, don't bother. He is no trouble. He is a stranger to the town."

"Come here," thundered the visitor.

Budshah quietly moved towards him. As he came near, madam very formally introduced the man to Budshah. "He is Maulana Noori, Chief of Kashmir Fund in Pakistan and Maulana Saheb, he is my guest."

"I am Zain-ul-Abidin," Budshah said with a regal flair.

"Which country?" enquired Maulana.

"Kashmir," Budshah simply murmured. "Oh you are from Kashmir—which Kashmir? Our Kashmir or their Kashmir?" persisted the Maulana. Budshah looking straight into Maulana's eyes and with all the confidence at his command said, "Kashmir is only ours."

"I like that, but young man, with such a good physique, what are you doing here?"

"I was simply passing by," Budshah replied.

"That is fine, but are you trained? Why don't you join our *Tanzeem?* I will send you to Afghanistan for higher training. But if you already possess the training in warfare then you can cross over to Kashmir with our men. In fact, only tomorrow we are sending a group—would you join it?" Maulana enquired. Budshah thought for a moment as if unable to comprehend. But finally he said, "I would join anybody who goes to Kashmir."

"That is fine. Then you will come with me right away. I will hand you over to the group Commander."

Maulana was enthusiastic. Budshah replied, "I am ready."

❖❖❖

Mahaballi had dozed off in his chair. The cassette had long ago run its full length. The phone in his shirt pocket rang and he woke up with a start. "Hello," he murmured into the phone and listened carefully. He heard and finally dismissed the caller. He remained seated, thinking. Finally he stood up and walked up to the cupboard. He opened it and brought out his briefcase. Placing it on a nearby table, he opened it. Searching through the contents he brought out a Sherlock Holmes cap, a long coat, a cane and a cigar. Mahaballi picked up these things and went to his dressing room. After a few minutes, attired as Sherlock Holmes, he walked out of his suite. His eyes were hidden behind the dark glasses; the brim of the detective's cap covered his nose too. He took long strides in the lobby of the hotel and looking right and left saw that the lobby was empty; even the receptionist was missing. He stood there in front of the counter puffing at his unlit cigar and playing with the cane.

The outer door leading into the garden was wide open and no one was in attendance.

Mahaballi thought for a moment. Where had the people gone? he wondered. But then in a flash it all became clear, and he began feeling happy. He hummed, '*Awara Hoon... Awara Hoon... Gharbar nahin... mujhko kisy say pyar nahin*'. The local television was to telecast Raj Kapoor's film *Awara* in honour of the visiting Mahaballi. People were glued to their television sets. But Sherlock Holmes had to take precautions. Therefore Mahaballi decided not to use the door but to jump out of the window. He walked up to a window, looked at it carefully, sizing it up in his mind. It was wide open. He went to the next. Yes, this was shut. So he dropped himself down near it and putting his hand into a pocket brought out a thick wire that had been turned into a hook at one end. He lifted the wire and putting its hook in the window latch pulled and pulled till it gave away. Mahaballi pushed the window. It opened with a cracking sound. He became alert. His hand, already in his pocket, fondled the revolver. But no one appeared to have heard the sound. He stood up and looked out of the window. The garden was quite empty. He pulled himself up and then onto the window. He took stock of the situation inside and outside. Satisfied, he lowered his weight and let go. He fell on the ground with a thud. He remained on the ground for sometime not making a move. Finally he looked around.

It was quite safe, he thought.He decided to crawl along the entire length of the garden to reach the compound wall. He decided against using the wide open gate. He would scale the wall instead. After all he was Sherlock Holmes.

After an hour's hard labour Mahaballi was waiting for a taxi on the mainroad outside the palatial building. Traffic seemed to be off the roads. *Awara,* Mahaballi thought and felt good. At last a taxi appeared in the distance. It moved at snail's pace. As it neared Mahaballi, he gestured with his cane held out. The taxi screeched to a halt. Mahaballi turned his coat collar up, lowered his hat by another few centimeters and entered the waiting taxi.

Once seated Mahaballi ordered, "Fire." The driver gave a laugh but started his engine. The vehicle began to move. Mahaballi not satisfied shouted, "Fast...faster...faster."

The driver replied. "*Eh lo.*" Mahaballi heard, looked in the side mirror and saw a Sardarji. But he could not become friendly with him so he ignored his Punjabi and instead yelled, "Follow that car, fast." The driver looked ahead; there was no car. He turned his head and said, "Sir there is no car."

"Fast, go fast."

"But where do you go, Sir?" enquired the driver.

"Just go on."

"But where, Sir?" The driver persisted.

"When I don't know, how can I tell you?" The Sardar

was beginning to get upset. He murmured, *"Twadi Maa"* and pumped the accelerator.

Mahaballi heard the sound in his inner pocket. He brought out the phone and listened. "Yes speak."

Raw Kaw informed him that Birbal was on his way to the airport in the company of a beautiful girl. They were booked for the US. The plane was due to leave in half an hour's time.

Mahaballi switched off and put the phone back into his pocket and shouted. 'Airport…fast."

"*Ok, eh lo twadi maa di.*" The vehicle ran at breakneck speed and Mahaballi sat there enjoying the thrill.

❖❖❖

Ajab Malik entered yet another chamber in the underground. Here the light was dim but enough to allow one to find one's way through the rows of chairs that lay all over the place. The center of the area was raised in the form of a platform. Many people were already seated. He found an empty chair and slumped into it. Without any announcement loud music began. Ajab Malik tried to locate its source but it appeared to emanate from everywhere. Then a battery of lights came on and focused on the raised platform. Everybody waited with great expectation and then it happened. A gorgeous woman appeared from a corner and people made way for her as she passed. The moving lights picked her form and followed her as she walked leisurely towards the platform. She seemed to hold the ends of a few strings in her hands. A close look revealed that her collared pets followed her. As the women came onto the platform she pulled the strings and one by one her pets jumped onto the platform. They were young men naked from head to toe.

Collared round their necks they were on leash and as all three of them reached the platform they moved on their haunches. The lady stood in the center and the young men crawled to her. They began by licking her ankles, her legs and her knees. Then she removed her skirt altogether and they licked her thighs. They howled like dogs. The lady then removed her top. Her full breasts came into view. They hung on to her breasts, sucking, licking and growling. It went on and on. Unable to bear it any longer, the lady picked up a leather strap and began hitting her pets. This did not deter them. They went for her with renewed vigour. They barked at her and using their hands as their paws tried to claw at her breasts. In the melee that followed one of them went straight for her panty and holding it with his teeth tore it into shreds. As her hidden body was exposed all the three charged at it, barking, fighting and growling at each other.

Ajab Malik was in a stupor. He did not know what

to think. He did not know how to react. He turned his head around and saw that the entire assembly of men and women were frantically reaching for each other. It was an orgy in full swing. He was dazed. He did not know when the young girl sitting next to him had come closer. He could only see the top of the girl's head in his lap.

❖❖❖

Nullah Khan, the Supreme Head had broken the protocol by coming to the bus stand at Muzaffarbad to receive Yousuf Shah. As the bus coming from Rawalpindi drove into the stand the Azadi party volunteers raised pro-Azadi slogans. The bus came to a halt and passengers began alighting from it. The crowd waited expectantly looking at each face that emerged. After a while Yousuf Shah appeared. The crowd, which had till then been silent burst out, "We want Azadi."

As Yousuf Shah's feet touched the ground, Nullah Khan took a few steps forward and embraced his chief in the valley. It was an emotional reunion. Nullah Khan's father had served as a horseman in the Kashmir palace. When Yousuf Shah was a king, Nullah Khan had been drafted as his personal attendant. Times had changed and now Yousuf Shah was a crownless king. Nullah Khan had come a long way. Having been thrown out of the palace for stealing a horse from the royal stables, he had moved aimlessly in the countryside. It was during one of these aimless travels that he came face to face with Maqbool and his dream of Azadi. Maqbool went to the gallows and Nullah Khan ascended the throne vacated by him.

Khan enjoyed every bit of his new role. As he embraced young Yousuf Shah, he was aware of the challenge this young man could pose. He patted his shoulder and escorted him through the crowd to a waiting Cadillac. Yousuf Shah waved to the crowd and wanted to make a short speech but Nullah Khan held his arm and almost pushed him into the car. Once inside, Nullah Khan began to clear his throat. The driver started the engine and the car began to move. As it cleared the crowd and came onto the wider road Nullah Khan began, "Yousuf Sahib, I welcome you to this place." Yousuf Shah turned towards him, "Chief, I am really touched by the welcome." Nullah Khan shifted in his seat. He said, "You have to be careful. We have no friends, all are our enemies."

Yousuf Shah did not expect a serious discussion to commence immediately. He just nodded in agreement and this was enough. Nullah Khan began his monologue. "One attacks us from the front and the other from behind. We are sandwiched between two enemies. They are both usurpers. Both want to finish us. Sometimes I feel the smaller one is more dangerous."

Now Yousuf Shah had to say something. He stopped Nullah Khan with a wave of his hand. "Chief, listen to me. You have not faced what we are facing, so it will not be wise to draw conclusions." Nullah Khan was not used to criticism. He turned red. His eyelid flickered incessantly. The corners of his mouth twitched but somehow he held on. He became silent and still. Yousuf Shah looked out of the moving car. He could see tented hutments in the distance. Ah! Refugees. Refugees and more refugees, that too in one's own land. I too am a refugee he thought and shifted his gaze.

❖❖❖

Kalhan Pandit brought out his pen from an inner pocket. He looked at the pen, his faithful companion of fifty years. This was the pen that his father had bequeathed him along with the family heritage of genealogical tables. Kalhan Pundit's shaking hand steadied itself and slowly his composure returned to him. He sat there holding the pen in his hand. His tormentors waited expectantly. The sheaf of papers lay neatly stacked in front of him. As if in a trance Kalhan spoke to himself, 'I will never betray you. I will never compel you. I will never break you.' His captors were taken aback. One of them put his hand on Kalhan's shoulder, "Hey Pandit, what is this nonsense? Put your signature on the paper or be ready to die."

Kalhan Pandit seemed to listen to nothing. He continued to murmur, "I will never lose you, I will never misuse you." The young man shook his shoulder but to no effect. He looked at his companions, "What has got into him? Is he mad? Has he gone crazy?"

"No, no, he is just trying to fool us. He is a clever Pandit. You don't know them. He wants to wriggle out of this, but he can't. We will kill him straightaway. We have no time for his pranks."

"But will that solve our problem! If he dies we do not get his signature."

"Oh yes, that is a problem. Leave him for the present. Report to the commander. He will find a way."

They stood up and leaving Kalhan alone in the room moved out. Kalhan continued to stare at his pen. He lifted his hand and touched his forehead with it, then kissed it and said aloud, "Thank you. Thank you. You have saved me for the present, you shall save me hereafter too."

He suddenly felt a new resolve deep inside him. He would not sign. After all why should he be scared? He had lived a full life. He should be ready to die even if it was at the hands of these rogues. As if to translate his inner thoughts into action he stood up and moved around. He no longer felt his legs sagging, his heart pounding or his mouth dry.

Lally moved under the almond trees. Dazed, she looked at nothing. She simply continued to walk barefooted and totally naked under the loose and ill-fitting pheran. Her hair was disheveled and it flew all around. Her arms hung by her sides as she walked. One almond orchard ended and another began. She continued to move. A thorn gored into her sole but oblivious to the pain, she moved on. At last she came out of the woods and into a clear expanse of land on the bank of a beautiful lake. She stopped and moved her head. She looked at the lake, then shifted her gaze, moved her head and saw the shrine perched on a cliff by the side of a bare brown hill. Her feet moved and with her stare fixed on the shrine she continued to take small steps. After going some distance, the flat and plain ground gave way to a steep terrain. Lally kept on moving. She rammed into the rocks, she stumbled against the boulders. She fell here, she fell there but she continued to move. Her gaze remained fixed on the towering shrine. As she inched her way her feet bled, her naked legs were bruised. Her pheran got entangled in a thorny bush but she moved on carrying all the thorns on her garment and in her soles.

It was almost evening when she finally arrived in the marbled courtyard of the grand mausoleum. The mausoleum of a saint revered by all.

Her bleeding feet left blood marks on the glistening marble tiles. A flock of pigeons stood in her way but oblivious to their presence she continued to move and reached the beautifully decorated entrance. There she could see the sanctum sanctorum. One glance at it and she slumped into a heap on the floor. The few men standing around saw her going down. They rushed to her and carried her away into an adjoining area. They brought her into a small cabin and placed her on the floor. An elderly lady, a nun living at the shrine was called in and she took charge.

❖❖❖

Kashyap ruled over his newly acquired kingdom with an iron hand. State functionaries loyal to Jaladbhava were eased out of their jobs and loyal people imported from outside. Kashyap's own tribesmen were inducted. The entire system of governance was taken over by these fair-skinned, sweet-tongued intelligent men. The local populace was banished to meaner roles. Certain areas were earmarked as exclusive domain of the superior race, the ruling class. The natives had no rights—no right to freedom, no right to liberty of action and thought, or right to property; all rights were withdrawn. Special care was taken to discourage, and at times prevent natives from acquiring knowledge. Thus sat Kashyap on the throne of Kashmir. Jaladbhava's nation slipped into slavery although pockets of resistance remained, but over a period of time Kashyap overcame all that remained of native pride. He felt happy and contented too. He had achieved what he had sought. Kashyap had become possessive of his kingdom. So much so that he did not like the friendly intrusions of his benefactor, the great monarch Nilnag. The mistrust grew day by day and after sometime Kashyap was convinced that Nilnag was out to usurp his kingdom. Nilnag had been receiving reports from his agents. These reports pointed towards the change in Kashyap's temperament. But initially he had kept quiet. As reports of more serious nature continued to pour in, he decided to act. He called one of his senior ministers and discussed the whole affair with him. It was concluded that the senior minister would travel to Satisar as a special emissary of Nilnag and sort out the differences. Kashyap was duly informed. But on the appointed day Kashyap chose to be away from his palace. The meeting could not take place. The minister returned to *Pataal* disgusted and disappointed. Nilnag was furious. How could he, a protege of Nilnag get away with such brazen defiance? After all it was he who had landed his troops and got the country for Kashyap. Nilnag decided to teach Kashyap a lesson. He called his secretary and dictated a long letter. The letter was in the form of a *firman* addressed to Jumbo. Listing Kashyap's acts of omissions and commissions Nilnag concluded that Kashyap and his tribe were not fit to rule directly. He and his tribe could however be excellent as officials of the state. Making this important point, Nilnag invited Jambo to take over the kingdom. He offered all help.

❖❖❖

Ajab Malik entered the technology center. It was a dream come true. Here he was to realize his lifelong ambition of learning the intricacies of the most cutting-edge TV technology. It was a grilling schedule. He had all along been a dreamer, cozily ensconced in literature and fine arts. At first the world of technology had appeared to be totally alien to him. He felt he was an outsider who knew nothing about the basics of technology. But the course managers had worked out a complete schedule taking all his deficiencies into account. He had to go through fundamental courses in physical laws, optics, electronics and a host of other related subjects. As he went through these courses, a new fascinating world opened up to him. For the first time, he became aware of the dynamism of matter. The basic laws governing physical processes could be interpolated into meta-physical situation. The basic and fundamental features of entire thought process looked to be the same: knowing the unknown. Physicists were essentially philosophers. Their only distinction was in the degree of stress laid upon the rational. Philosophers created their own norms to test the hypothesis propounded whereas scientists tried to test their theories on universally accepted and acknowledged standards. The philosopher's logic attained mathematical precision in science. All considered, philosophy could be, while science was. Ajab Malik reflected on all these issues. The philosophical background forced him to dive deep into the newly acquired bits of knowledge.

Basic beauty of matter lay in its simplicity of organization and complexity of form. A stone and a log of wood were essentially the same. An atom was the basic unit and indivisible under ordinary circumstances. Combinations and permutations based on simple methods resulted in the great diversity of forms. The change was eternal, continuous, and self-propelling. Dynamism seemed to be the order. Learning about the attributes of matter equally fascinated Ajab Malik, especially the indivisibility and indestructibility of it. And then that marvel which ran through the entire universe in a never-ending cascade, the energy, changing its forms but never ceasing to be.

There was not much to be discussed with his tutors. They were essentially interested in creating a scientific temper in this young man before pushing him on to more complicated areas of electronics and optics. By and by Ajab graduated from one course to another. His tutors were impressed with his sharp intellect and extremely good memory.

Vision was the conduit or the bridge that connected the human mind to the outside world. The eye was projected as a complete and perfect camera, taking in the minutest detail presented to it in its visual field. The mechanism of picture formation, the role of nerves, the importance of a screen to project the picture was very clearly brought out. Then there was the super computer, the visual cortex inside our brain that received inputs from a host of sources, decoded them and then controlled and guided the entire operation.

Dr Speilberg was the master of simulation. He could recreate intricate mechanisms with the help of his gadgets. He had organized a demonstration of mechanism of vision, using a high-grade camera, which could automatically rotate around a 180 degree plane and take pictures, which were directly transferred to a TV screen. The entire assembly was linked to a super computer, which was programmed to alter the description of the pictures. Ajab was amazed to see the results being projected on the TV screen in front of him. Dr Speilberg continued with his discourse, explaining the different modes of his gadgets. Ajab Malik raised his hand. His teacher noticed it and encouraged him to ask his question. "Doctor, is our memory also linked to vision? I can see whatever I select from the storehouse of my memory?"

"Yes, Ajab Malik, you are right and see I have simulated

that also. We have been running this equipment for sometime now and everything that has come into the camera has been stored in the computer. Here push this retrieval button and you get a choice of one million bits. Now whichever bit you want can be brought on to the screen. So simple."

Ajab Malik was ready with yet another question. "In that case, Doctor, can't we go for partial simulation. Say, you use my memory in place of the computer's stored memory and display the same on the screen for all of us to see."

Dr Speilberg was impressed, "That is right, that is possible and I think we can try that. I will think over it. Do see me later. We can discuss this idea. It seems quite logical."

Dr Speilberg left his students there. He straightaway headed for his room. Ajab Malik had thrown him a little challenge and he was eager to overcome it.

❖❖❖

It was a group of thirty young men. It included eleven Afghans, five Sudanese, six Arabs, two Bangladeshis and five local guides hailing from different parts of Kashmir. Budshah made up the thirtieth of the group. Their leader was a burly Afghan, Abu Kendal Gul Bahar. He was to be addressed as Amir. All others were brothers, brothers in Islam all fighting for a common cause, the cause of Allah. Barring the five locals and Budshah, no one had been to Kashmir. They were brought together a few days before their planned departure and made to know each other. Rules and regulations were made known. A strict adherence to a code of conduct was expected of them. The Amir took the opportunity to renew and rekindle the flame of Jehad. He spoke well. Budshah felt impressed. On the appointed day, they set out early. A bus took them from their guesthouse to the Karachi railway station where seats for them had been booked in advance. They carried minimum luggage. They were told that once in Kashmir, the local populace would provide them with every item of comfort.

Inside the train the Amir sat in their midst. He signaled to them to come close and listen. He raised his hands to join them in front of his serene bearded face and said a short prayer, "Oh Allah! The master of earth and heaven, the master of the Day of Judgement, listen to our supplication. We, your subjects, turn ourselves to thee. Oh Allah! accept our offerings. We, your humble servants, pray to thee. We come from thee and we shall return to thee. Allah lead us on in search of our goal for it is thee that moves us on. In battle may we perish, accept our Jehad and reward us on the appointed day, the Day of judgement and forgive us all our sins. Oh Allah! Be with us, Amen."

The congregation surrounding the Amir responded by raising their hands and saying, "Amen".

The train journey had begun and Budshah, sitting in a window seat, could see the evening descend over Karachi. Tall skyscrapers were receding as the train accelerated on its tracks. He continued to stare into the night, lost in his own inner world. He longed for his beautiful Kashmir. This hot sultry evening reminded him of the pleasant and cool environs of his palace, nestled between majestic chinar trees. Budshah wanted to return to his land. He had seen enough. He had traveled enough. He had thought enough. A plan was shaping up in his mind. A plan that envisaged establishing a united, bold self-confident Kashmir. A land where all lived in eternal peace, where no one was discriminated on the basis of his creed, his faith. His Kashmir was to be a state firmly dedicated to the development of human intellect in all its manifestations. Budshah continued to think of ways and means to achieve his goal—the goal of total enlightenment, emancipation and prosperity.

❖❖❖

As the taxi screeched to a halt outside the airport, Mahaballi jumped out and ran into the building. Coming into the departure lounge he dashed for the counter. The beautiful girl looked up at him enquiringly. Before Mahaballi could interact with her someone touched his shoulder. He turned and found Raw Kaw standing obediently in front of him.

"Your Excellency, he is through, heading for the aircraft. Your plane is ready; this way please."

They ran through the long corridor that opened directly on to the runway. There Mahaballi could catch a glimpse of Birbal escorting a beautiful girl on the aircraft staircase. He ran to his own aircraft, which lay parked at a distance. As he reached it, the pilot received him and guided him up the stairs into the plane. In a moment the plane began to move. Mahaballi stretched his exhausted body and the hostess began giving him a massage.

Mahaballi picked up the phone and instructed his pilot to follow Birbal's plane. Satisified at the piece of good work, he relaxed. The massage helped a lot. As the plane soared up into the sky, Mahaballi drifted off into a slumber. The hostess woke him up. Mahaballi looked furious, "What is it?"

"Sir, it is important. The captain wants to speak to you." She handed him the cordless phone. Mahaballi said, "Yes."

"Sir, the plane that we are following is changing its course. It is not heading for the United States, that is America. It is instead going towards Africa."

"Africa ? What the hell does Birbal intend to do there?"

"Sir, I don't know."

"Ok, continue to follow him and keep me informed."

Mahaballi handed over the phone to the waiting hostess. He was wide awake now.

'What did this mean? Birbal, Birbal you are a pain in my neck. I will thrash you. I will show you your worth but let this treasure scam end.'

Mahaballi continued to feel agitated. After a flight of more than four hours the captain of the plane contacted him again.

"Sir, we are following our target. He is landing in Burkino Faso—are we to land?"

"Burkino Faso?"

"Yes Sir, that is the name given by the ground control. They want us to identify ourselves before we land."

"Burkino Faso, Captain. I haven't heard of it. Are you sure we are on the same planet?"

"Yes Sir, we are."

"Ok, seek the permission. We will land. Give them our identity."

"Yes Sir."

As the plane began to descend, Mahaballi readied himself for the impending state welcome. After all, he would not be taken lightly by a nondescript country.

The plane came to a halt on the runway a little after Birbal's plane had taxied to a halt.

Mahaballi stumbled upon an idea just before he was

to come out of the plane. "Captain, request the ground control and security to secure the passengers of Birbal's plane. They should be asked to take Birbal and his girl into protective custody. Of course, in case they have some law like TADA it would be excellent."

Then Mahaballi appeared at the head of the stairs.

The president of the Republic of Burkina Faso, Major Odom was present along with the country's tribal chiefs dressed in local custumes. The members of a tribal dance troupe were busy gyrating their half-clad bodies and a band played the national anthem. Mahaballi inspected the guard of honour and was driven to the only elite hotel in the city. On arrival there he enquired about Birbal. His hosts informed him that it was not possible to arrest Birbal because the lady accompanying him happened to be an American. Mahaballi was fretting and fuming. He enquired about their whereabouts. He was told that Birbal had also checked into the same hotel along with the girl. Mahaballli saw a ray of hope. He would shortly confront Birbal and force him to part with the treasure. He went into his suite and made himself comfortable. He lay on the bed fully stretched. The exhaustion was beginning to take hold of his senses. He never knew when he dozed off.

It was midnight when he finally awoke. Suddenly coming to his senses he realized where he was and what ought to have been done. Without wasting any more time, he got up and walked out of the room. A guard had been posted outside his door. He was asleep. Mahaballi woke him up and asked him about Birbal's room. The guard pointed towards an adjoining suite. So close, Mahaballi thought. He straightaway went and pushed the door. It was not bolted. Mahaballi was cautious. He put his hand into his pocket and brought out his revolver and walked very slowly. He could see nothing. He fumbled for the switchboard and found it on his left. He pressed the button. The room came alive with a dazzle. Mahaballi took a good look around. He saw Birbal lying prostrate on the bed. He was totally naked. No one else was in the room. He walked towards the bed where Birbal lay. His eye caught a sparkle on the floor just near the bed. He looked intently and bent to pick it up. It was couple of gold coins. He felt them with his fingers, held them up and turned them to see the details. On one of the coins he could make out the engraving of a royal head. He turned it over. He could read the words engraved in Persian script, *the Sadr-e-Riyasat*. He looked at the other coin. It too had a head engraved and the motif on the reverse read *Wazir-e-Azam*. He pocketed the coins.

He was beginning to lay his hands on the treasure. Good, he thought and went near the sleeping Birbal. He called out to him. There was no response. He shook him by his hand; there was no response. Is he alive or is he dead? Mahaballi was frightened. He again looked around. He spotted a neatly folded paper on the bedstead. He moved a step and picked it up. He unfolded it and read aloud.

'My dear Buffoon! You proved to be a bit hard. But now I have the last laugh. By the time you wake up I will be in the States. I am taking away all the coins. I have no use for your cards but I could not tear them off my pants though I tried hard and tore many in the process. Goodbye! Be happy. I am leaving the pants for you. It will remind you of me and of course the cards may be of some value to you. Ha! Ha!'

Rachel

Mahaballi looked around and spotted the denim jeans lying in a corner. He picked up the jeans and had a close look. They were inside out and Mahaballi could see the cards glued to it. Some lay in pieces on the floor. He sat down and began picking up the pieces. Having secured the last piece he got up and carrying the jeans he left Birbal's room and headed for his own suite.

In half an hour's time, Mahaballi had arranged a broadcast to his nation. He sat there waiting for the crew to arrive. It did and the whole country waited with bated breath for the extraordinary broadcast. As the cameras were fitted, lights were on and the crew chief shouted "action", Mahaballi began to speak to his countrymen.

"We speak to you from a faraway land, thousands of miles away, from Africa. We have laid hands on the treasure that was being smuggled out. However hard though we tried, we could not recover the entire treasure. But my dear simple people of Kashmir we must rejoice for we have with us two coins which we offer to those who win a little game, the rules of which shall be framed very shortly. It is a game of cards. Instead of fifty-two cards we have seventy-five. You know there is one referee for soccer, two umpires for cricket but this game will have three. We request the people of Kashmir to play this little game so that peace and prosperity, jobs, power, apples and above all rice become abundant. We are confident that the people of Kashmir will rise to the occasion, Jai Hind."

❖❖❖

Yousuf Shah had a number of sessions with Nullah Khan and his aides. The more Yousuf pondered over the discussions the more suspicious he became. Nullah Khan was perhaps maintaining a carefully cultivated facade. He seemed to have abandoned Maqbool Dar's dream. Behind all the rhetoric of freedom and unification, he seemed to be hand in gloves with the policy makers of the host country. Yousuf continued to think as he sat in the lavishly furnished guest room of Nullah Khan at Muzaffrabad. At last he came to a conclusion. He had to recast his policies. He could not continue to live under Nullah Khan's protection for long. Yousuf Shah felt that he had a commitment to his people and to himself. Both seemed to be unsafe under the prevailing arrangements. He resolved to immediately set out for his land. He would go back to his people, work with them and explore all the possibilities for a settlement. If Nullah Khan, the chairman, could live in peace with the usurpers on this side of the dividing line, why could he not make his own peace with the usurpers on that side? After all, how long would he continue to be on the run, long for the majestic chinars, the Dal Lake and above all his Khatoon? Yousuf Shah became emotional. He could see Khatoon roaming the saffron fields of Pampore in search of her beloved.

❖❖❖

Lally was within the shrine's premises. The old hermitess had nursed her back to life. Her wounds were healing fast and the constant care and cajoling put her on her feet. She began by taking a few steps inside her room but, by and by, she regained her strength. Her mental state, however, remained unaltered. She continued to stare aimlessly and move with a wooden posture. She did not respond to any commands. She seemed to be beyond the reach of any intrusions. The hermitess took pains to keep her neat and tidy, feeding her with her own hands and attending to her every little detail caringly. It was a moonlit night and the hermitess tucked Lally into her bed. The autumn chill was beginning to acquire a cutting edge. The old lady was particularly concerned. She did not want the poor girl to catch a cold. That would definitely retard her progress. She took extra care in covering her with an additional blanket. Satisfied that the girl would be comfortable, the lady left her room and came to the adjoining one, where she used to stay, praying through the night. That had been her practice for a decade that she had till then spent at this shrine. She came to her chosen spot in the adjoining room and sat facing the Kaaba and closed her eyes. The holy verse sprang to her lips, "*Allah-o-Akbar.*" Immediately she seemed to be transcending into another world, the world of her inner self where nothing existed except "Allah." The lady sat there suspended in oblivion.The night moved at a leisurely pace, the moonlight illuminating the mountain tops and diving deep into the valley below. The marble dome of the shrine spread light all over the hillock.

The darkness withdrew towards the corners of the small room unable to challenge the angelic light emanating from her being. The dim moonlight sneaked into the room and bestowed a glow upon her white face. The *chadder* covering her head made up the halo.

It was then that the stillness of the night was shattered by a terrible shriek. The agonizing cry almost pulled down the wall between the two rooms. The hemitess shot up and sprinted towards Lally's room. As she flung the door open, she could catch a glimpse of the hem of a robe going out of the window and dissolving into the night outside. Undisturbed Lally lay in her bed. The hermitess went close to her. She saw that the girl was quietly sobbing; a stream of tears was rolling down her cheeks.

❖❖❖

Ajab Malik sat in the special chair that Dr Speilberg had designed. An assistant brought a helmet and placed it carefully on his head. A bunch of wires connected the helmet to a battery of instruments placed behind him. A large screen was placed at some distance in front of Ajab. Dr Speilberg checked the entire assembly of gadgets. His students stood in a circle, keenly observing every move that their teacher was making. Having satisfied himself, the doctor cleared his throat, raised his hand and said, "Now Ajab Malik be ready. As soon as I push this green button you will close your eyes and concentrate on one subject—anything from your past. Remember, whatever you retrieve from your memory will appear on the screen. So better be precise. Avoid jumbling your memories. Okay, are you ready?"

"Yes doctor, I am ready," replied Ajab Malik.

Simultaneously, he felt somewhat uneasy but kept his calm. Dr Speilberg called his students to attention and then began counting 10, 9, 8, 7, ... 3, 2, 1. He pushed the button on the panel in front of him. Ajab Malik closed his eyes and searched his memory for something to produce here. The excitement was so intense that he was unable to pick up anything for a while. The screen remained blank. Then it began, first a haze, slowly a blur and then a picture. The entire group watched with bated breath as a beautiful crystal clear lake surrounded by snow-capped mountains appeared on the screen. A small boat materialized on the placid waters. A man, a woman and a little boy sat on a thick mattress. The man looked taller than the mountains around him—serene, calm, composed, lost in his own world. The woman played with the little boy and brought out a candy; the little boy removed the covering and hastily put the candy into his mouth, played with the wrapper and then tossed it into the lake. The woman reprimanded him, warning him by gesticulations. The lake became turbulent, waves and waves all around the little boat. The little boy clung to the woman's bosom as the boat rocked, turned and tossed; the man sat calm, quiet and serene. Ajab Malik opened his eyes. Dr Speilberg pressed a button. The entire audience came alive. The doctor hurried towards Ajab and putting his hand on his shoulder exclaimed, "Congratulations Ajab Malik, we have done it. We have done it. Wait, I will play it back to you." He walked back to his panel, pressed a key and looked up at the screen. It remained blank. He waited. The entire audience waited. Ajab Malik waited but nothing happened.

Dr Speilberg checked his gadgets. He fiddled with the keys on the control and a caption appeared on the screen "Disc is blank."

"Oh my God! I didn't connect the recorder." Everybody watched in disbelief. But never one to give up or give in, Dr Speilberg said, "Never mind boys, we have done it. We will do it again. Ajab Malik, do stay awhile."

The doctor again went through the entire exercise. Ajab again closed his eyes shut as the doctor pressed the key. The screen came alive with a lush green meadow. There appeared a backdrop of a dense forest and a range of lofty mountains. A big bird of multicoloured plumage descended from the skies and landed on the outstretched palms of Ajab Malik. Dr Speilberg and his students watched spellbound. The screen froze and Ajab opened his eyes. Dr Speilberg pressed a key. The screen went blank. He got up and moved towards Ajab. He felt concerned. "What is it Ajab Malik. Are you well?"

"Yes, doctor, I am alright."

"Then, remove your helmet, come out and join us, and we will play back now."

Ajab abandoned the chair and joined his friends.

Dr Speilberg headed for his panel and played back the sequence. Ajab watched and as soon as the bird appeared he ran towards the screen calling out loudly, "Noshlab, my Noshlab! Noshlab, my Noshlab! Where are you? Where are you?" Dr. Speilberg and his students ran after him. As they came near, he became dizzy and numb, and mumbling incoherently fell on the floor in a heap and passed out.

❖❖❖

Dr Speilberg heard Ajab Malik with full attention. When he finished his tale, he tried to rationalize the entire sequence of events. "Look Ajab, it could simply be a case of autosuggestion. You have lulled your senses into believing that a charm was thrown at the young lady and she was transformed into a unique bird. Your mind has not only given it a shape but also provided it with wings to fly so that it has gone away. What you need is psychiatric help. We will arrange that. But before we do that, let us be certain about one thing. This bird of yours," he pointed towards the large screen where a bird stood projected, "needs to be tracked. We can do that. I will feed it into our super computer, establish a link through satellite and scan entire Germany. We will try to locate any bird resembling this one. That shall satisfy you?"

Ajab Malik heard the good doctor with patience. At

last he replied, "I am not mad. If only you knew what I know, and if only you had seen what I have seen, you would believe every word I spoke. But I do agree, it is hard to believe in such seemingly impossible stuff. I will gladly submit to a psychiatrist but as you said, "Let us go for the scan."

"That is fine my boy. Here we go." Saying this the doctor got up and so did Ajab. They headed for the super computer chamber. Once inside, the professor began his elaborate exercise of feeding the data into the computer. Ajab watched in silence. Turning towards him, the doctor said, "Let us begin with the entire planet. Let us issue a command. Is this type of bird a native of the planet?" He fiddled with the keyboard in front of him and typed out the command. In a few seconds the screen went blank and Ajab Malik's heart lost a beat or two. The screen came alive and in bold words, he could read, 'Yes.'

"Good," said the Doctor. "Now our next command." He began keying it in.

'Is it a native of Europe?'

Again the screen went blank and again after a few moments it brightened up and a definite 'Yes' emerged on the screen. "Good... Good," said the doctor. "Now my boy, I am going to frame a critical command!" He began keying in again. 'Is this bird a native of Asia?'

'No,' the computer readily replied. The good doctor

turned to Ajab Malik. "There you see. If it were not a native of Asia, how come you saw it in Kashmir?"

Ajab Malik's face lit up. His story was beginning to gather evidence. He shrugged his shoulders. The doctor looked back at his desk. "Now let us go for the scan, or wait a bit, let us get some more information." He began keying in the command. It read 'What is the total number of this species in Europe and how is it classified? What are its characteristics?' Both men waited for the computer to process the information and come up with answers. It took some time. Ajab fixed his gaze on the little screen in front of him. By and by, the words emerged.

'There is only one bird in entire Europe that is unclassified. Not in store.' Dr Speilberg almost fell off his chair. He turned towards Ajab Malik. "It is a great mystery. I am beginning to believe you. Come let us go to the scan. We cannot leave it at that." They rose from their seats and proceeded into an adjoining chamber. It housed the great marvel of scanning technology. A set of innocuous machines was capable of scanning the entire globe for the minutest of things. This was one of Germany's prestigious creations.Within a fraction of a second, the person sitting behind the panel could locate the tiniest of villages, streets or buildings situated anywhere on the globe. Dr Speilberg took his seat behind the panel. He switched on the unit and a screen flashed in front of them. He was so preoccupied with the idea of locating the bird that he almost forgot Ajab Malik who stood behind him. The doctor fed the complete data pertaining to the bird and commanded the unit to scan Europe for it.

The scan came to life and began working immediately with a buzzing sound. The doctor waited and Ajab Malik's heart began pounding in his rib cage. His sixth sense told him that Noshlab was at hand. He could smell the fragrance of her hair in the still environs of Dr Speilberg's laboratory. For him time stood still. He remained at the threshold of a new dawn. Deep inside him he knew that all his dreams were going to come true. The scan continued to roam over the vales and dales of Europe, over soil and sea, over forest and meadow, over rock and bush, over busy highways and waterways. It was an eternity for both the men sitting behind the panel. At last the buzzing sound stopped and the screen came to life. The camera took a shot of a thick forest with green, tall, beautiful trees, against the backdrop of high snow-capped mountains. There was a lush green meadow in the foreground with flocks of sheep busy grazing. The camera zoomed onto the trees and continued to hover over them, scanning almost every tree. "Jesus!! It is there! Yes, it is there," Speilberg burst out having spotted the bird perched on a tree. Ajab could not believe his eyes, "Yes, yes, there's my Noshlab, there.... He could not complete the sentence. He was totally overwhelmed. His voice choked, tears streamed down his cheeks. The doctor put his hand on the keyboard and commanded, 'Exact location of the spot.' As soon as he wrote, pat came the reply: 12 miles NE Lat....

The doctor issued another command.

'Zoom in on the object. Full view all angles.'

The scan began to operate but the camera seemed unable to project further. The doctor repeated the command. Again the buzzing sound came on but the cameras refused to go beyond a point. "What is wrong?" the doctor murmured to himself. Ajab Malik's gaze remained glued to the screen where he could see his Noshlab perched on a branch. At last the answer to the doctor's command appeared.

'High energy field around the object—not possible—further progress not advisable—damage to system apprehended.'

"Oh my god! Ajab Malik, your bird is really mysterious to say the least. You talked of a charm or something?"

"Yes she was transformed into this shape by a wicked Baba. I told you that."

The doctor thought for a while. Then he again began typing out a new command.

'How to break the energy barrier?' Pat came the reply.

'Fire high energy beam in the outer ring of objects energy zone'

Dr Speilberg was not sure now. How could he fire a

high-energy beam from his station? Ajab Malik was now on edge. He did not want to lose Noshlab again. He began pleading with Dr Speilberg. "Please do something for God's sake, please."

"I can understand your situation. I am beginning to believe in you, let us see. We will try our best."

He began working on the panel giving commands and receiving replies, analyzing them and framing new questions. It took a lot of time to come to some conclusion. At the end, the doctor had resolved to break the energy barrier surrounding this unique bird. He postulated that once the barrier was neutralized, a more favourable situation would emerge. He wasn't sure, but nothing else could be done. He began preparing the high-energy beam. He worked out the entire sequence. The beam would be fired from his laboratory but before that it was necessary to transport Ajab Malik to the area where the object was situated. He could be of immense help as the new situation arose. He devised the entire plan and discussed the matter with some of his colleagues over telephone. Ajab Malik readily agreed on the condition that Noshlab's safety would not be jeopardized.

Ajab Malik set out on his journey to the woods. Dr Speilberg had established phone contact with him while he drove on the highway. The doctor wanted him to calm his nerves. He was monitoring the entire operation from the laboratory. His scan had picked up Ajab's car and he waited for the moment Ajab came closer to his goal.

❖❖❖

Misra Begum was all alone in her palatial house at Muzaffarbad. Time hung heavy on her. What should she do? She picked up the remote control of her TV, pressed a button and the screen in front of her came alive. PTV was telecasting a documentary on Kashmir. She had seen it a number of times. Same processions of men and women, soldiers in battle dress, military convoys, freedom fighters, wailing women, shots of martyrs, the ever increasing graves in the graveyard. Misra Begum switched off the television; reclining on a divan she closed her eyes. Her childhood memories surfaced in her mind. She was a little girl sitting in the company of her classmates in a small dingy room, the window overlooking the Jhelum river. The teacher, a bearded turbaned Maulvi Saheb was reading from a book and the children recited after him. She clearly recollected the lines. *Yeh tamanna hai ki apni ma ki soorat dekh lun.* (My only wish is to see the face of my mother).

It was a poem, titled *Lament of a blind girl.* Misra Begum opened her eyes. Her mother. Ah! Her mother!

Misra Begum had not seen her mother for the last forty-four years. She was born in a large family. They were five sisters and two brothers. She was the youngest. Her father was a maulvi who led prayers in the local mosque. His disciples lived in far off countryside. Each morning he would attend to the needs of those who had faith in his spiritual powers. He would listen to them one by one, write a Taweez or simply recite a few verses and blow his breath on the afflicted. His followers had great faith in his healing powers and touch. Everyone pampered Misra,her being the youngest child in the family. As she grew up, a British nun started a girl's school in the vicinity. The entire clergy was up in arms against this move. As the lady disembarked every morning on the banks of the river, people ran into their homes, and tightly shut the doors and windows. The lady just smiled and took the few steps that led to her school. In the beginning only a few girls from Kashmiri Pandit households attended her classes. One day the lady was found knocking at the door of Misra's father's house. As the word spread in the household that the Mem Saheb was waiting at the door, Imam Saheb considered the situation. What should he do? He could not risk the wrath of the authorities, that too of the Sahebs. On the other hand, welcoming the lady would amount to blasphemy. As Imam Saheb fretted and fumed, the little devil Misra ran the entire length of the courtyard and opened the door for the Mem Saheb. The lady was pleased. She picked up Misra in her arms and came in. Now nothing could be done. Imam Saheb beckoned his Begum to receive the lady and escort her into the house. A curious horde of onlookers gathered in the courtyard of Imam Saheb's house.

The Mem Saheb was very forthright. She straightaway declared, "Look Imam Saheb, I have come to discuss the girl's education with you. I hear you are a great Islamic scholar, well versed with the scriptures."

The Imam wiped the beads of sweat from his face and brow and said, "Please sit down."

'What does the Holy *Quran* say about it?" The lady confronted the Imam with a specific question. He sat there. He did not know what to say. The lady continued, "Is it true that the Prophet's own wife is considered as one of the greatest Islamic scholars?"

"Yes," the Imam Saheb managed to say.

"Would it be possible without the education she received from the holy Prophet himself?"

"No."

"Then what is the basis for denying education to these wonderful girls of yours?"

There was no escape for the Imam Saheb. At the end of this first encounter, the Imam had consented to allow the youngest of his daughters, Misra, to join Mem Saheb's classes.

Misra Begum's chain of thoughts was abruptly broken by a knock at the door. She got up from her comfortable seat and moved across the length of her sitting room. She opened the door and seeing the visitor, a young lad living in the vicinity, smiled at him and beckoned him in. Misra Begum was reminded of her only son whenever she came across a handsome young man. Her son was away in a country in the Gulf, earning petro-dollars. Her daughters, four in all, had been married off and lived in different cities of Pakistan. The boy came in and Misra Begum followed him. As he sat, she enquired,"What would you like to have son? A cup of tea?"

"No *khala* nothing. I only came to tell you that a group of Mujahideen is leaving for the valley tomorrow. You wanted to send something there. Anyway, two Mujahids will spend the night in your guest room. You can talk to them."

"So kind of you, my boy, to have remembered. I will eagerly await their arrival. When shall they come?"

"By evening, I was told."

Saying this the boy stood up and took leave. Misra Begum showered all blessings on the young man and saw him to the door.

As she returned to her seat, tears welled up in her eyes. Kashmir. Ah, those mujahideen were going to Kashmir—her mother—her Kashmir.

Kalhan Pandit continued to hold his tormentors at bay. His eccentric behaviour had earned him some reprieve. He was in no mood to relent. His captors tried hard to bring him to his senses. He would at times behave quite normally but as soon as his captors mentioned a pen, Kalhan Pandit would feign a possessed state of mind. Left to himself, he would think of ways and means to end this captivity. He could, however, never reach any conclusion. There seemed to be no way out. He had tried everything. He had pleaded with his tormentors. He had gone on a hunger strike, only to ask for food after three days. Having got used to him, his captors had lowered their vigil. Occasionally he would be allowed the luxury of coming out of the secluded hut and into the open yard through which ran a shimmering stream. There were a couple of poplars planted on one side and a majestic chinar stood on the other. On one such excursion, he saw a young man squatting on the green turf by the side of the brook. A copy of the holy *Quran* stood on a wooden stand in front and the youth recited from it in a rich voice. As Kalhan came nearer, he could see tears rolling down the cheeks of the youth disappearing into his thick beard. The young man saw him and stopped reciting. Kalhan beckoned him to continue. The young man hesitated but Kalhan with folded hands pleaded, "Son, please continue, I would bartar my life for listening to these holy words, they soothe my soul. Please read."

The young man smiled and resumed his recitation. Kalhan sat behind the young man in all humility and devotion. After a while the young man stopped reciting. He began reading aloud the translation of the verses he had recited.

"He is Allah, other than whom there is no deity, knower of the unseen and the witnessed. He is the entirely merciful, the especially merciful. He is Allah, other than whom there is no deity, the sovereign, the pure, the perfection, the bestower of faiths, the overseer, the exalted in might, the compeller, the superior. Exalted is Allah above whatever they associate with Him.He is Allah, the creater, the inventor, the fashioner; to Him belong the best of names. Whatever is in the heavens and earth is exalting Him.And He is the exalted in might, the wise."

As the young man paused for breath Kalhan picked up from him, reciting from his memory the shaivite mantras he had learnt when he was a toddler "He is self radiant, self-sufficient, self-dependent, self-explanatory, self-conscious and self-evident. He is all that exists and that does not exist and yet He transcends the whole phenomenal universe. He is all pervading and transcends the physical barriers of time and space. Everything is in Him and He is in everything. All this is mere manifestation of his own powers brought about by his supreme will. It is a long and continuous drama wherein He plays different roles though apparently looking various characters. But actually, it is His and his show alone. When this reality dawns upon an aspirant, he attains true knowledge. He becomes an enlightened soul, a liberated soul. He becomes one with Shiva and virtually merges in Him by getting dissolved in that boundless luminosity, he utters in great ecstasy 'Shiva Aham.'

The young man looked at him in awe. Kalhan spoke as if in a trance. His whole form seemed to be transformed. Words coming from his lips appeared to emanate from his soul. As he stopped, the young man got up and came to him. "Panditji." He touched his shoulder. Kalhan seemed to wake from a slumber. He opened his eyes, took a look at the dazed young man and said, "My son, if only people knew, we quench our thirst from the same spring."

❖❖❖

Lally moved out of the shrine's premises very quietly. No one knew as she ran down the flight of granite steps while the first rays of the sun emerged on the eastern horizon. Her dishelved hair flew in the morning breeze. Her legs moved at a frenzied pace, oblivious to the danger of falling on those hard granite steps. In one go she descended all the steps and reached the dirty patch of road at the bottom. Here she paused for a while, turning her head and casting a longing look at the shrine perched above on the rocky precipice. She moved on humming to herself. She did not know where to go. She just moved and with every step, the melody within her grew. The initial humming transformed itself into a reverberating song. She continued to walk and sing. Early pilgrims to the shrine saw her as they crossed her in their path. No one took any particular notice of her and no one understood a word of what she sang. Lally came into a thickly populated area. With the arrival of the morning, human habitation stirred. People began coming outdoors to fulfill their daily chores and saw her there. She went on singing hymns no one understood. A lady standing in an open door saw her advance. She called out to her, "Come here! Have some tea." Lally stopped at the door. The lady went inside and returned with a cup of steaming salt tea and some snacks. Lally sat there and drank the tea. The lady enquired, "Where do you come from?"

Lally just looked at her and smiled. The lady sensing that the woman possessed some supernatural powers persisted. "Why don't you come in?" Lally got up and resumed her walk. The lady called but Lally seemed not to listen. She was on her own journey, singing her own incoherent, unintelligible hymns. She ate what people offered her. She drank what they held out to her. She walked during the day and took shelter anywhere during the night. By and by, she came to be accepted as part of a routine. No one bothered. No one seemed to worry on her account. She continued to roam, singing her own hymns, till one day when she was arrested by the Mujahideen and charged with obscenity, vulgarity and unIslamic ways. People watched as she was handcuffed and paraded through busy streets and taken to the Mujahideen hideout. No one intervened. No one protested. No one recognized her. No one claimed her. No one owned her. People just watched as silent spectators. Her arrest provided them with yet one more topic for gossip. Some said she was an agent of RAW. Some said she collected information about the Mujahideen during the day and briefed the security forces at night. Lally, handcuffed, was produced before the Chief of "Ulema council". A young man with a black beard on a heavy face sat at an exalted position as Lally, drawn and weak, with dishelved hair, wearing a pheran which was in tatters, stood in front of him. The council members, seven in all, stood in a semicircle, three on each side of the chairman. They were all bearded men, sporting caps of various shapes. Apart from their beards they shared a common vulture like gaze, devouring the weak bundle of flesh presented before them. A man rose and announced, "Sirs, here stands a women who brought faith into disrepute by her actions. She moves about half naked. She does not cover her head. She does not fast when prescribed. She freely mixes with men. She sings in public. She performs her vulgar dances on the roadside. She is produced in front of you to receive her punishment in light of the holy word, and Sharia. May Allah be merciful upon us, Ameen." All those present responded with 'Ameen'. The chief of the council took a long look at the subject of discourse standing before him and addressed her thus: "I seek Allah's help against Satan, the wicked. In the name of Allah, the most merciful, the most compassionate,praise be to Allah and Muhammad, the seal of prophets, Peace be upon him. Khatoon you have heard the charges that have been made against you. Before pronouncing our judgement we give you an opportunity to defend yourself. Say what you may, we are listening."

Lally who had hitherto been humming very quietly broke into a loud pitch. "When fish shall fly, the birds swim, flowers bloom in embers, mules pen verses and asses paint. When fish shall fly, the birds swim, flowers bloom in embers,...." The council chief looked at the jury. His deputy sitting next to him said, "Chief, I think we are wasting our time. You should deliver your judgement." The jury supported the motion with one voice and the chief cleared his throat and said, "In the name of Allah, the most merciful and beneficient. In the present case against anonymous Khatoon, it is proved that charges have been made on the basis of sound evidence. Therefore, in accordance with Sharia, it is ordered that she be stoned till death. May Allah's mercy be upon us, Ameen." And Lally continued to sing, "When fish shall fly, the birds swim, flowers bloom in embers, mules pen verses and asses paint. . . .”

❖❖❖

Gani roamed the wilderness. He looked for his companion under the dense almond trees, along the banks of the lake and over the top of the hillock. She was nowhere to be found. As darkness began to crowd around the trees he hurried his steps, looking down from the raised plateau. He saw the entire city shrouded in a mist, the sun having gone down the western mountains.

He concentrated on the scene in front of him. Nestled among the multitude of houses stood the shrine. Its pinnacle rose above the layer of mist. Gani continued to walk. Night was descending fast and darkness was engulfing the city. The air seemed to be still and the trees motionless. A deadly silence prevailed and only Gani’s footsteps made the difference. As Gani came down to a level ground, the distant barking of a dog became audible. Gani had lost his tracks. He had lost his companion and, in search of her, his own course. He continued to walk aimlessly. After walking for an eternity he stopped. He could see nothing. It was pitch dark all around. He sat down, feeling with his outstretched hands the turf under him. He remained there suspended, motionless, lost in an ocean of darkness. Suddenly he heard a distant roar, a thunder in the sky, he thought. He looked up towards the sky. He saw swarms of particles glowing in the heavens. The thunderous sound deepened into a roar. Gani stood up, unable to comprehend. He continued to gaze at the glowing particles, which seemed to cover the entire city sky. He shivered in horror as these glowing objects spewed fire over the city. In a flash, the entire city shone. He found himself in the courtyard of the holy shrine. The deafening roar had gained a monstrous intensity. Gani fell to the ground shaking under his feet. He steadied himself and lunged towards the shrine door. The skyline turned brilliant as thousands of fires raged all around. Gani could see rising flames trying to reach the sky.

He ran for his life. There was no way one could save oneself from the fire that seemed to engulf everything. Gani saw chinar trees catching fire and turning to ash in no time. He continued to run, trying to avoid the explosions in his way. The rattling sound echoed, the big bangs shook the earth and seemed to tear the crest of the ground. The leaping flames produced so much heat that water in the hitherto placid Dal began to boil and houseboats on its surface flew up into the sky. Gani ran through the fire and heat, death and destruction. His own robe caught fire more than once and he burnt his hand extinguishing the leaping flames. His beard was singed and he could smell the smoke that filled his nostrils. He ran on as people ran from one end to another, only to be consumed by a falling block of building or an explosion under their feet. He saw them trampled under mountains of debris. He could do nothing but run away. At last the spray of fire began to wane and it was all quiet. Again the night was as still as the inside of a grave. Gani looked hard. The leaping flames were at a distance now. In the reflected light he could recognize his own house, half-burnt but still standing on the banks of Nalla Mar. Gani ran towards it stumbling on the debris from razed houses. He reached his home and went inside closing the door shut and secure behind.

❖❖❖

Yousuf Shah conveyed to Nullah Khan his intention of crossing over to Kashmir and his desire to be with his people. After all, he was the last recognized Sultan and it did not behove him to desert his people at this critical juncture. Nullah Khan opposed the move, basing his argument on concerns for the safety and security of Yousuf Shah. He argued that since Yousuf Shah was the rallying point for all freedom fighters, he could not be exposed to the dangers connected with his return to the battlefront. Yousuf Shah dismissed the argument and declared that he would not be held back by any real or imaginary threat to his life. Nullah Khan then tried the political card. After all, the host country would be offended if symbols of Kashmir's freedom and resurgence were to abandon the great Islamic State and choose to live under the umbrella of the *kufar*. Nullah Khan thought that it would amount to a negation of the two-nation theory and set in motion the long disastrous chain of regional aspirations fuelled by identity crisis. But Yousuf Shah was firm in his resolve. He would not be stopped at any cost. Nullah Khan sensed that Yousuf Shah actually could not be stopped and submitted to him, but at the same time pleaded that he be given the responsibility of organizing the travel. This would allow him to draft and detail trusted bodyguards to ensure the Chairman's safety and security. Yousuf Shah relented and Nullah Khan set out on his mission. He had to raise a contingent of trustworthy fighters at short notice. Taking leave of Yousuf Shah he headed for his office and once there he closeted himself in the secret inner chamber where two hot lines were available. He picked up one phone and was directly connected to the chief of RAW in Delhi.

"Hello!"

"Namaskar chief," Nullah Khan said and smiled as he heard the reply to his salutations. Then resuming he just mumbled few numbers into the mouthpiece.

"56207 by 2 upon YXZ."

Again he smiled into the mouthpiece, gave a short laugh and said. "Ok ji, Namaskar."

Replacing this hot line, he picked up another telephone and was directly connected to the chief of ISI in Rawalpindi. "Hello! *As-Salaam-Alaikum.*" He listened and smiled into the mouthpiece and said, "85293XYZ upon ABC. *Achha jenab. Khuda Hafiz!*" He replaced the receiver and sat on his chair. A sheet of paper lay in front of him. He brought out a pen from his pocket and began putting down names on the paper.

The escorting contingent of Yousuf Shah was going to consist half of RAW and half of ISI men.

❖❖❖

There was a knock at the door. Misra Begum was all ears. She had been waiting all evening for the Kashmir bound Mujahideen. She had made arrangements for their dinner. She opened the door and there stood two of them. "I am Zain ul Abidin," Budshah said and pointing towards his companion continued, "He is Abdul Bari from Sudan." Both men saluted Misra Begum and she showered her blessings upon them and ushered them in. Once seated, she spoke, "I was delighted to know that you are on your way to Kashmir, though I have not seen Kashmir for the last four decades." She turned emotional. She tried to hide the tears that were welling up in her eyes. Budshah sensed her anguish and said, "Sister, we can understand your plight.

It is very painful to live away from Kashmir. We have the experience. Please tell us what we can do for you."

Misra Begum had by now controlled herself. She smiled at Budshah and replied, "Oh,what a fool am I! You must be tired. You have a long journey ahead of you. You should not engage in idle talk."

"Oh no, nothing of the sort. We are very happy to see you and know that you are so concerned about your motherland."

"Mother—Ah Mother, my mother." Misra Begum suddenly became oblivious to her immediate surroundings and as if speaking in a trance continued, "My mother, lonely mother, old and infirm, sick and helpless, my mother, my mother Kashmir—If only I could come to you, if only I could secure you from your loneliness...."

Budshah listened in total silence. His companion Abdul Bari turned to Budshah, "Eh brother, what is wrong?"

Budshah signaled him to keep quiet. Misra Begum continued, "My mother, lonely mother, sick and infirm mother, old and helpless mother...."

Now Budshah intervened, "Sister, sister." Her chain of thoughts was suddenly broken. "I am sorry. I could not control myself. Please forgive me. I have gone crazy." Budshah pleaded with her, "We wish we could be of some help to you. Please tell us."

Misra Begum gave in and began, "Yes brother, my

mother lives in Kashmir, totally helpless, sick and old. There is no one to take care of her. Her sons have been consumed by the Jehad. All my sisters have died. What can I do? Oh my God what can I do for her?" Budshah could feel the pain growing in his own heart. He felt miserable and could not utter a word. Abdul Bari wanted to say something but could not as Misra Begum, wiping her tears, continued, "I want a favour from you. I have packed some warm clothing for my mother. It doesn't weight much; I know you have a rough journey ahead. Could you carry these clothes to my mother? She will not suffer the chill. Could you?"

"Yes, yes, we will carry them even if they are so heavy as to break our backs. We will carry them for our mother," Budshah said as a couple of tears rolled down his cheeks too.

❖❖❖

Ajab Malik stopped his car on the edge of the road cutting through a lush green meadow. Dr Speilberg instructed him over phone about his future course of action. He abandoned his car and walked towards the distant forest. He knew his Noshlab was there perched on the bark of a tree. Dr Speilberg had warned him of the energy barrier that had been detected around the mysterious bird. Ajab increased his pace. He was breathless but he continued to run. As he neared the woods the doctor came on the line. "Look Ajab, slow down now. Don't disturb the bird. It may take off." Ajab slowed his run. He walked slowly now. He knew that his ordeal was about to end. He was coming face to face with his destiny. He had suffered a lot. She too had suffered a lot. As he came close to the trees the doctor was again instructing him on the exact course he needed to follow. He turned on his left and walked ten paces.He was to turn right and after another twenty paces turn left and stop. As he stopped, he looked around him. He could only see the fir trees. He scrutinized every tree with utmost care.Where was she? His heart pounded in his chest. His legs began to sag. He was totally overwhelmed by emotion. He located her. There she was. Yes, Noshlab the mysterious bird sat there perched on a branch. Ajab Malik froze. The doctor came on the line. "Now Ajab! Sit down quietly and cover your eyes. Do not look at anything as we fire the missile to break the barrier. You will hear a bang. Once it is over, you get up and look straight ahead of you—towards the trees, where the bird sits."

The doctor went off line. Ajab went down and prostrated on the ground. He covered his eyes with his hands and waited. Ages seemed to pass. He remained in supplication waiting for the magical moment, the moment which would change his life, which would deliver him from his pain. At last he heard the bang. He felt the ground shaking under him. He was terrorized and desperate but he controlled himself. He remained still. The roaring sound ceased. The ground under him became still and he could hear the chirping of birds. He felt relieved, but then a scare ran through his bones. Noshlab? Where would she be? Was she well? He opened his eyes and leapt to his feet. He stretched his neck to look ahead of him. He saw in the distance that a girl sat reclining against a tree. From the distance Ajab Malik could not make out the features. He took a step, then another, and another. He continued to move forward, expectant, and at the same time hesitant. As he took the eleventh step, the listless form reclining against the tree shook her head, the dark cloud of hair shielding her face parted in the middle and Ajab Malik called out, "Noshlab, Noshlab, my Noshlab," and ran the remaining distance into the waiting arms of a smiling Noshlab. Dr Speilberg watched the proceedings from his laboratory. As he saw the mysterious bird disappear in thin air he remarked, "The bird is dead."

❖❖❖

Nullah Khan had made all arrangements to see off his chairman.

A guard of honour, a twenty-one gun salute, everything was in place. Yousuf Shah inspected the guard of honour and took the salute at the parade. Then taking leave of Nullah Khan, he boarded the car that was to take him to the last post. A dozen vehicles teeming with his bodyguards, all men in uniform and heavily armed escorted his car. As Yousuf Shah's motorcade passed the hilly streets of Muzaffarabad, people lined on either side showered petals and raised slogans, "Chairman Zindabad—we want Azadi." Yousuf Shah smiled to the waving men, women and children and began thinking of the hazardous journey he had undertaken. He had a lurking suspicion of Nullah Khan. He could not trust the men Nullah Khan had drafted for his protection. Who were they? Yousuf Shah had no idea. He had to take the risk. After all he had to reach Kashmir. He resigned himself to his fate, closed his eyes and rested his head on the back of the seat. Except for the driver he was alone in the car. They traveled for a long time. He became sleepy. He did not know when the car had come to a halt. When he opened his eyes he saw a few men trying to wake him up. He came out of the car. He was told that the car journey had come to end and now they were to go up the mountains.

The last post was a few hours away and it would be dusk when they reached there. Yousuf Shah was taken into a nearby house where lunch had been laid out. He ate along with his guards and then set out on his long march. They had to hurry so that they reached the last post in time. It was a tortuous journey up the steep hills and across deep gorges. Yousuf was a fit man and he kept ahead of the others. His guards fell behind him a number of times and he had to stop and allow them to catch up with him. As the sun went down the western peaks, they reported at the last post. A major of the Pakistan army welcomed Yousuf Shah in customary style. Yousuf replied to his salutation and the major escorted him into the post. The army unit had prior information and they had prepared a brief for the visiting dignitary. The Major took him into a bunker and educated him on the secret route that had been chosen as safe passage for Yousuf Shah's travel. As the two men pondered over the route map, the sound of gunfire erupted outside.

Yousuf Shah sprang up in his seat. The Major signaled him to sit down. Yousuf Shah asked, "What is it? Major!"

"Oh! Don't worry,it is a routine exchange of fire. Both sides enjoy it. No harm intended."

Yousuf Shah sat down and they resumed discussing the travel plans.

❖❖❖

Abu Kendal Gul Bahar was a considerate man. He went out of his way to make the members of his group comfortable. They were going up a mountain. It was a very steep ascent. They had to move on their haunches, taking cover under the thick bushes that grew in abundance in the area. Their local guides had warned them of the vulnerability of this route. The enemy picket was only a few peaks away and with night vision devices their movement could be monitored. They had chosen this route for this was the shortest route available. They moved very cautiously and Abu Kendal would stop after every few yards to satisfy himself of the progress of the most sluggish of his climbers. They carried heavy loads mainly comprising of ammunition and weaponry. Each member of the group carried a fully drawn AK-47 and had been kept on maximum alert. As a bright moon shone in the sky above, Abu Kendal and his men completed the ascent. They had reached the top of the mountain and there lay the valley of Kashmir down below. Even in the faint moonlight they could not miss the breathtaking splendour of this paradise on earth.

Budshah too looked down at the valley below. He felt a renewed vigour overtaking his tired limbs. He was in a divine mood. His own country was finally in front of him. His country, that beautiful country! Abu Kendal also saw the splendour and grandeur of the valley. So this was it! Well such beauty always did ignite passions in jealous men. But it was the territory of Allah and he had set out on a holy mission, the mission to reclaim it for Allah. They called it paradise and paradise could never belong to infidels, he rationalized. They took a break. Their guides were happy, as they were no longer sitting ducks on the steep slope of the mountain. They could now defend themselves in case an exigency arose. They had their food and leisurely began to descend into the valley. It would be an easy descent. Their men would be waiting in the little village, the contours of which were visible from the height.

By daybreak, the group had reported at the village mosque. The village folk had already assembled at the mosque, and after morning prayers, Abu Kendal and his men accompanied the village elders into the village. Their aching bodies had been relieved of the heavy burden as volunteers gladly carried their bags.

They were escorted into a capacious house and entertained to a sumptuous breakfast. Abu Kendal began to interact with the locals. He enquired about the prevailing situation. He was told of the large-scale arrests being made. The daily encounters between freedom fighters and Indian forces, and the periodic strikes in the cities. While talking to the village elders, he noticed that Budshah was not present at the breakfast. He enquired about him from his men. No one seemed to know. Well he would be somewhere, maybe talking to one of the folks outside the house. After all, he too was a local. Abu Kendal got over his anxiety and continued to gather information about the happenings in the valley.

It was quite late in the evening when it was concluded

that Budshah had indeed given them the slip. A search was launched in the village but it was fruitless. Among the locals, no one seemed to remember him. Abu Kendal and his men got jittery. Could he possibly be an informer, an enemy agent? Abu Kendal recollected that Budshah had in fact appeared to be quite mysterious. He would not talk much. He blamed his own judgement. After all, he was the leader. He should have suspected. After a lot of discussion it was concluded that the group should abandon the village as soon as possible and move on, before Budshah reached there along with the enemy's troops. They had a hurried dinner and set out on their journey. Abu Kendal had to trust his guides. He was apprehensive but he could not desert them. He was in an unknown land and unfamiliar with its treacherous ways.

❖❖❖

No one in the group noticed that Budshah did not enter the mosque but continued to walk straight ahead. He crossed the tiny village and came into the open paddy fields. Greenery soothed his eyes and a constant cool and fragrant breeze invigorated his soul. He was in a joyous mood. He continued to walk. He crossed the vast expanse of green fields looking intently at the paddy fields with interest. A good harvest was at hand, he judged. He came into another village. There too stood a little mosque in front of him. He went inside. People had lined up for the morning prayers. Budshah joined the last row. As prayers were offered, the village folk noticed a stranger amongst them. A village elder approached him as he was coming out of the mosque. "Stranger, may God's blessings be upon you," he said.

"Upon you too," replied Budshah. Both men came out of the mosque. The villager picked up the conversation. "Sir, times are difficult. We do not know a friend from a foe."

Budshah kept silent.The villager asked, "Sir, who are you? And what brings you to this village?"

"We seek our own men, we are passing on." Budshah's reply was too much for the simple villager but he concluded in his mind that the stranger was 'one of them'.

"Sir, forgive me for my inquisitiveness, but please do come with me. Stay a while. Have your breakfast."

"No thank you. God be with you. We have to move on," Budshah replied and moved on. As he left the village, he could not help but notice that almost the entire village had assembled and was watching him with awe. Word had spread fast that 'one of them' had visited the village.

Budshah continued to move from one village to another, from one hamlet to another, in search of his men. He was the Messiah in search of his lost tribe. As he came face to face with the villagers, he searched their faces, he analysed their attire, he examined their behaviour and moved on, till at last one day he arrived at an open meadow nestling between the woods. As he crossed the wide expanse of the meadow and was about to enter the woods, he heard voices that came from the woods. He went in and there they were. A group of men sat around a fire and talked amongst themselves. They did not notice the intruder. Budshah sat quietly among them. The man sitting in front of him turned, saw him, and sprang to his feet.

"You!" Yousuf Shah exclaimed.

"And you," Budshah, holding his ground, replied.

❖❖❖

Kalhan had finally found a supporter among his captors. The young man had been captivated by Kalhan Pandit's philosophy. As days passed, the young man grew close to him. Both men could be seen engrossed in philosophical discussions. As their relationship grew, the young man considered Kalhan's plight. 'Why was he in captivity? After all, what wrong had he committed?' He concluded that it was not only unjust but inhuman too to hold an old and infirm man hostage. He decided to help him escape from his captivity. As he let Kalhan know this, Kalhan took him aside and confided in him. He told him that he had already worked out a plan for his escape. He would, however, need the young man's help to succeed. The young man was already eager to help him.

Kalhan unfolded the plan to him. "Look my son,what I need is a dozen sleeping pills. You can help me in arranging them from the market whenever you visit one. Say, on Friday, when you go to the town mosque for prayers. You can go to any chemist's shop and buy the pills for me."

"What would you do with the pills?" the young man enquired.

"Do not worry, son, I would not kill myself with an overdose, be sure of that.' Kalhan responded to the young man's fears.

"I still do not understand,"pleaded the young man. "I will tell you at the right moment. For the present, you only try to arrange them. Once you do that, I promise I will let you know everything." Kalhan Pandit promised and the young man assured him that he would do everything to see him free.

Next Friday, the young man went to the town mosque for his prayers and Kalhan eagerly awaited his return in the evening. As the young man appeared in the distance, Kalhan knew that he would be a free man that very night

The young man handed over the packet to Kalhan who thanked him profusely, hugged him and kissed his forehead. "My boy! I will never forget this act of kindness."

That evening as the food was being prepared for the

Mujahideen guarding him, Kalhan entered the kitchen and started a conversation with the cook. Soon he had made himself comfortable in the kitchen. He waited for the right moment. As the cook went out to fetch some firewood for the hearth, Kalhan quietly got up and emptied the packet of sleeping pills into the boiling contents of a vessel on the hearth and calmly walked out of the kitchen.

❖❖❖

Yousuf Shah's guards surrounded Budshah. Dozens of AK-47 rifles pointed at him. Yousuf Shah intervened, "Do not bother. He is a friend." The guards lowered their guns and dispersed. Yousuf Shah moved a step towards Budshah and with a reassuring smile began, "Where have you been all these days? You disappeared at Karachi Airport. I looked for you."

Budshah did not reply immediately. After a while he said, "Let us not talk about who abandoned whom."

Yousuf Shah put his arm around Budshah's shoulders and both men began strolling around. Yousuf Shah's tent was pitched at a distance. As they reached it, Yousuf invited Budshah inside. Budshah hesitated for a moment but looking at Yousuf s pleading eyes moved in. They sat down and one of the guards brought their dinner. They had rice, with roasted birds that the guards had killed during the day. Over dinner, Yousuf Shah talked of his plans to join his people in their quest for freedom. He had resolved to lead from the front. He also gave an account of his sour relations with Nullah Khan and the apprehensions he nursed with regard to the guards provided by him. Budshah remained silent throughout the dinner. Afterwards, as both men washed their hands and reclined inside the tent, Yousuf Shah remarked, "You are an enigma. You do not talk. After all what do you want?"

At this Budshah sat up straight, and for the first time in centuries opened his heart to Yousuf Shah. "We are no enigma. We have nothing to say. We are overwhelmed by the misery, the pain that surrounds us. We have always strived for an honourable place for our people on the face of God's earth. We have a dream. You have asked as to what we want. We want to develop a prosperous, self-confident, bold, modern nation fit to take its place in the comity of nations—a nation free of hunger, disease, and ignorance. A nation that is tolerant, humane and just. We want each man to respect other men, without reference to caste, creed, faith and religion. We want education, healthcare, sanitation, power, industries, hospitals, bridges, roads, factories, airports, science, technology, computers, satellites, electricity and we want electronics. We want to preserve our ethos, our culture, our language, our woods. We want to preserve the Dal lake, the chinar; we want to preserve the Hangul, we want to preserve all our shrines, we want to preserve Hazratbal and we want to preserve Tulmula. We want all this and much more." Budshah seemed to be in a trance and his words came to Yousuf Shah as if from a distance. Yousuf Shah felt each word cutting through his being. As Budshah fell silent, Yousuf Shah touched his hand in a gesture of supplication. The tent appeared too small. It could not hold these two men. Suddenly Budshah had grown in size. He appeared as a giant and Yousuf had to strain his neck to look into his eyes. He could see the sadness and pain of an entire people crystallized in Budshah's eyes. Yousuf Shah could take it no more. He stood up and suggested a stroll in the cool environs of the woods outside.

As they came out into the open, they passed the tent where off-duty guards rested. They heard some voices and moved nearer. Someone was talking over the wireless.

"Yes Boss, we will do that. But, what to do with the body? Over."

The person at the other end replied, "Feed it to vultures or do what you like, but kill Yousuf Shah, over."

"Sir, the RAW men may want their pound of flesh."

"Saw his body into two and give half to them."

"Right boss—one more thing, one of his friends has joined him."

"Friend? Now, who is this?"

"He calls him Budshah."

"Oh him, kill him too, but wait, you kill Yousuf Shah, let RAW kill Budshah, but kill them both, over and out."

Yousuf Shah and Budshah were terrified. Both men were in the jaws of death. Yousuf Shah's own bodyguards were plotting to kill him.

"Oh treachery! Oh, conspirators! Oh God! What a day!"

Yousuf Shah lamented.

"It is not day, it is midnight. Let us make good our escape while the woods are dark," Budshah said.

Yousuf Shah was already moving from there. They walked cautiously trying to move very quietly. They could not risk detection. As they gained some distance, they threw all caution to the winds and ran.They ran wildly without caring for the difficult terrain. They ran on and on. They wanted to go as far as they could before dawn.

The guards came to know of their escape in the morning. The Commander immediately contacted Nullah Khan and informed him of Yousuf Shah's treachery. Nullah Khan was furious. He directed the guards to fan out into the woods and search for the missing men. Nullah Khan contacted Delhi and arranged for a massive manhunt.

The army columns situated in the area were put on the job and the army commanders drafted 'friendlies" into the countryside. They had to locate the two men, arrest them and kill them in an encounter.

Yousuf Shah and Budshah continued to run from one forest to another till they came into the open meadows. Traversing the meadows they entered small sleepy villages, and finally reached the outskirts of a town. It was evening time. The sun was fast disappearing beyond the mountains. Both men felt exhausted. Unable to move, they took shelter under a chinar tree. Looking around they noticed a pond with a multitude of fish swimming in the placid waters. An old dilapidated temple stood nearby. Yousuf Shah and Budshah stretched their bodies on the soft turf. They never knew when they were engulfed by swarms of butterflies, their tiny delicate wings lulling their senses into a deep sleep.

❖❖❖

Kalhan Pandit's captors had their dinner and within a few moments they had fallen asleep. He examined each of his guards. Having satisfied himself he moved out of the small house that had held him captive for a few months. As Kalhan came out into the yard outside, he stopped for a while. He remembered his friend, the young lad who had helped him organize his escape. Unfortunately, he too had to be put to sleep. Kalhan headed for the spot where this young man lay. He went near him, sat on the floor, put his hand over the young man's head and kissed his shining forehead. He was overwhelmed by emotions. He wished this man well. He tore himself away from the sleeping youth and moved out. He had no time to waste. He had to escape in time. Coming out into the open, he began his march. He knew the direction he had to follow in order to reach his place. He had decided to visit the tiny room from where he had been kidnapped. He would collect the genealogical tables, the only treasure he possessed, and move out of the valley. His sons had been right. He alone had misjudged the situation. He would board a bus for the plains. Kalhan Pandit accelerated his pace on familiar ground. He had visited this area a number of times. He knew every villager of any importance. But he decided against knocking at any door. Times had changed. A friend was no longer a friend. Kalhan took a deep sigh.

Suddenly he felt as if he was traveling in an alien land. The trees under which he passed appeared different. The mountains in the distance seemed strange. The ground under his feet appeared to oppose him. He felt surrounded by numerous faceless forms. He could sense their presence. He could see them dance around him. He could imagine them carrying drawn swords. Kalhan wiped the sweat from his brow. He reassured himself. These trees, well, they were the same.

There is my favourite tree, the chinar, and there stands the Pir Panchal range of mountains. I have grown up under its benevolent gaze from my childhood. An oppressive silence engulfed him. He continued to walk. He could hear a lonely dog barking in the distance. He began humming a mantra. This would calm his nerves, he thought. By and by, Kalhan Pandit managed the long distance, and at dawn, he stepped into the sprawling temple complex. He had to hurry, get his papers, and move out. As he traveled the wide expanse of turf under the trees, he saw his favourite chinar at a distance. He could not resist the temptation to have a closer last look at the tree planted by his ancestors. He changed course and headed towards the majestic chinar. He came near and held his breath as he saw two men lying prostrate on the green turf beneath the tree. Kalhan remained there, motionless. He did not know what to do. Who were these young men? Both looked regal in appearance. They were no ordinary mortals. Kalhan could not ignore their presence. He had to investigate. Who knew if these men had come from some far of land in search of him to get back to their ancestors. Kalhan could not deny them the right to know. He moved nearer. He was no longer scared or confused. He touched the shoulder of one of the men and called out softly, "Hello, please get up, I am back."

There was no response. He touched the other man and repeated his words. The second man opened his eyes, looked at Kalhan, took a look around and sat up. The first man also opened his eyes and sat up. Now Kalhan was in full control. "You both get up.You have been lying here, you could catch a cold. One of the men replied, "Thank you for your concern, we are fine."

"All right, all right, now tell me your name, both of you, then I will look into my tables and give you the entire information."

"Well, I am Yousuf, Yousuf Shah."

"And yourself?" Kalhan asked the other man. "Sultan Zain-ul-Abidin Budshah."

"Oh my God! What have I been doing, stupid me, I couldn't place you!" Kalhan Pandit prostrated himself in front of the two. Both men looked at each other. Budshah put his hand on Kalhan Pandit's head and said, "Rise, Pandit ji. It doesn't look nice. You are an old man. We respect you. We hold you in high esteem, please rise."

Kalhan Pandit got to his feet. As he straightened up, a volley of bullets hit the chinar tree and twigs fell down in front of them. The rattling sound of AK-47 rifles spewing fire came from the entrance to the temple complex. Kalhan Pandit said urgently, "Sir, please come with me. You are in danger. There is only one place where no one can reach you. Please hurry to the storeroom behind the temple building. There, amongst my rolls and rolls of genealogical tables we shall remain and no one shall ever find us there. Come Sirs, come...and follow me."

Saying this, Kalhan led the two young men along the bank of the fish pond and behind the dilapidated temple building into his dungeon and hid them behind rolls of genealogical tables as guns boomed and grenades exploded outside.

❖❖❖

Doordarshan had purchased the global rights for telecasting live the grand Kashmir auction. The organizers of the auction were 'Kashyap and Sons Pvt Ltd' He had finally got around to accepting the DD offer. There was stiff competition with all the international networks in the fray. Ajab Malik appeared on the small screen. He was to conduct the entire show. He began by introducing Kashmir to his viewers. In chaste Persian he recited:

"If there is a paradise on earth, it is this, it is this, it is this."

He gave its geographical location as the camera focused on a world map and then an aerial view of the picturesque valley came into focus. He narrated various historical facts—the snow covered lofty mountains, shimmering lakes, singing brooks, waterfalls, and deep and dense woods engaged the viewer's attention.

The camera then moved to the airport. A Pan Am flight was taxiing and as it came to a halt, the Wazir-e-Azam accompanied by his cabinet colleagues and high officials waited in attendance. Miss Robin Hood emerged from the plane and descended the steps quickly. She was profusely garlanded by the Wazir-e-Azam as a multitude of men and women held at bay by baton wielding soldiers shouted, "Miss Robin Hood...Zindabad." The Wazir-e-Azam introduced the visiting dignitary to his cabinet colleagues and officials. The chief of All Parties No People Conference (APNPC), chief of religious and social organizations—all profusely welcomed the lady. Next the camera shifted to the waiting press persons. In reply to a question Miss Hood said, "We maintain that auction will pave the way for more dialogue between Kashmiris and Kashmiris. We still hold the right to declare the territory as a disputed piece of land."

The camera again shifted to an incoming plane. Maharaja Keran Rajput emerged from it and the great number of men and women present shouted slogans, "Sri Sarkar Zindabad." The Wazir-e-Azam welcomed the Maharaja and introduced him to his colleagues. In reply to a question the Maharaja said, "Our ancestors possessed the land, we have duly executed the sale deed. Our rights cannot be denied. We are the rightful owners. Usurpers must go."

The camera again shifted to an incoming plane. Mulla Nateg Shirazi in a black flowing robe and a round turban emerged from the plane and taking majestic strides descended down the stairs and was embraced by the Wazir-e-Azam who introduced him to the nobles who had been waiting. The men and women raised slogans.

"Inqilabi Islam Zindabad." Mulla Nateg Shirazi in reply to a question mentioned that there existed great similarities between his country and Kashmir so much so that "Shiraz is located in downtown Srinagar."

The camera again focused on an incoming plane. As it taxied on the tarmac, comrade Rinchan alighted from it and was received and profusely garlanded by the Wazir-e-Azam and his colleagues. The multitude of men and women raised slogans *Kishmiri Chini Bhai Bhai.* The camera focused on the incoming dignitary as he fielded questions from the press. He replied in his own language, which no one understood.

The camera again shifted to an arriving plane and crowds cheered as they saw a green flag with a crescent fluttering on top of the plane. The men and women went into raptures as they deciphered the PIA logo embossed on the tail of the plane. The multitude surged forward raising slogans. *"Pakistan Ka Matlab Kya? La ilaha illallah."* The baton charging soldiers brought out their guns and fired into the crowd. The camera shifted to the plane and a fully uniformed General Akram Khan Bhatti appeared at the top of the staircase. He saluted the men and women awaiting his arrival and descended the steps in martial fashion. The Wazir-e-Azam received him and introduced him to his colleagues and nobles. The chief of APNPC breaking protocol pushed the Wazir-e-Azam to a side and embraced the general. The multitude of men and women continued to be restive. The soldiers went on firing into the crowd and the camera shifted to the general replying to a question. He said, "The great leader's dream has to come true. We cannot leave our jugular vein in the hands of our enemies." The camera shifted to another incoming plane. As it taxied and the door was flung open a dhoti clad man sporting a khadi jacket and a white cap appeared and with folded hands saluted those present. The Wazir-e-Azam and his men received the man as he came down with hesitant steps. The multitude of men, women raised slogans, "Azad Hindustan Zindabad". The camera focused on the Mahaballi as he spoke to the press. "Bapuji had seen a ray of light and I have come to inaugurate a new power project.We will also inaugurate the work on a railway line connecting Jammu with Uri. Jai Hind."

The planes continued to arrive and the dignitaries, the bidders, the prospective lessees also continued to arrive as Ajab Malik reappeared on the small screen announcing a chhakri by Gul Akhtar and party. The direct telecast would be resumed as the bidders assembled in the international convention complex on the bank of picturesque Dal Lake for the greatest auction on earth.

❖❖❖

Gul Akhar's chhakri came to an abrupt end. The small screen went blank for a few moments. At last Ajab Malik's face appeared on the screen. The camera zoomed and the location came in view. Ajab was standing on Boulevard road with the international convention complex in the background. The camera again focused on Ajab Malik and he began to describe the atmosphere around the auction site. "It is a lovely morning. I can see the beautiful Dal Lake watching the proceedings silently. The Zabarwan hillock stands with baited breath. The chinar trees are listless as international bidders assemble in the complex. As you can see, children in school uniforms line the entire boulevard. As a motorcade passes they wave their little hands."

The camera then focused on the little children with blank expressions on their faces. They mechanically lifted their hands as a new motorcade appeared. Ajab then announced that now the telecast would resume from within the Convention Complex where the action was about to begin. The camera shifted to the inside of the complex. A large and capacious hall came into view. There stood a large round table with all bidders seated around it. Kashyap stood on a raised platform with the backdrop of Kashmir. A small working table with a hammer lying on its top was placed in front of him. Kashyap cleared his throat, tested the microphone, signaled his assistants who stood on either side and began, "Ladies and gentlemen, we are witness to the making of history. Today you shall decide the fate of this

Paradise on the earth. I am not giving you any statistics. All of you know the importance of this priceless property. The terms and conditions have already been circulated. As we begin this auction, we will allow every bidder to stake his claim to the property. I invite Miss Robin Hood to stake her claim."

All the bidders cheered as Miss Robin Hood stood up and began, "After the end of the cold war, we are the only remaining power in the world and it is our responsibility to take care of the underprivileged. Our heart bleeds when we see small children weaving carpets. We cannot allow this. Therefore, in order to stop this and also felling of trees and protection of ozone layer we lay our claim to this piece of land. We have already quoted our price and we intend to get it or else we have the veto power." Miss Robin sat down. Kashyap thanked her and called the next bidder.

"Maharaja Kern Rajput Hazir Ho!" TheMaharaja got up and reciting a few shlokas in Sanskrit came directly to the subject. "We have a sale deed, duly attested and certified. We have the strongest claim to the property. We must not be ignored. We are ready to double the lease amount, I mean, what we had paid then, we will pay double the amount today. Thank you."

As the Raja sat, Kashyap called comrade Rinchan. He stood up and talked incessantly in his own language. No one understood a word. He bowed and sat down. The auctioner thanked him and called Mahaballi to lay his claim. Mahaballi straightened his cap and stood up. "Namskar! With folded hands here I stand in front of you. We are ready with an economic package and a political package. Each package is a bundle of packages. The economic package has a power package, an employment package, a food package and so on, whereas the political package has election package, political process package, 370 package, Autonomy package, 52 package, 75 package and so on. We are the largest secular democracy in the world and we humbly declare that we will continue to defend Kashmir against the raiders, against the proxy war, *dhanyawad.*"

Kashyap thanked the Mahaballi and called Mulla Nateg Shirazi, who got up and reciting holy verses began, "The Satanic verses cannot be allowed. The greatest Satan will be opposed. Death to Satan. We will see to it that the revolution reaches every village and every home. We have a mission and we will accomplish it. Come what may Kashmir is part of the great crescent. It is the tip of it. We will have revolution here."

As Mulla Nateg Shirazi was speaking, Miss Robin Hood stood up and shouted at the top of her voice. 'We will not allow any rogue state to participate. We will use all our might to silence this voice." Mulla Nateg Shirazi, not to be outdone, responded more vehemently,

"Marg bar Shaitan, marg bar shaitan-e-buzurg."

Death to the Satan, death to the greatest Satan."

Miss Hood had by now lost her cool. She picked up her satchel and running through its contents brought out a lipstick. She applied fresh make up on her dry lips and then tossing the stick towards Mullah Shirazi said, "This is a ballistic missile. It will split your guts."

Mulla Shirazi snatched the briefcase from the hands of comrade Rinchan, opened it and brought out a matchbox. Bringing out a stick he threatened, "If I drop this stick all of you will melt. This center will blow up into the air and all will be over."

Comrade Rinchan looked aghast. Mahaballi stood up and so did Maharaj. As they tried to run away, Mulla Shirazi came in their way. They fell on each other. The matchbox fell to the ground. There was a big bang and the screen was covered with smoke. The camera shifted to Ajab Malik. As Ajab Malik looked towards the convention complex, it went up to the sky and split into thousands of pieces. The loud bang shook the earth. The placid Dal water went turbulent and the Zabarwan hills reverberated as the debris fell into the lake. Little children ran towards Ajab Malik and surrounded him. After a while, all was quiet. Ajab Malik took a look at the debris floating on the surface of water, and addressed the children, "Come children! Let us clean the Dal."

EPILOGUE

"These our actors, As I foretold you, were all spirits and Are melted into air, into thin air: And, like the baseless fabric of this vision, The cloud-capp'd towers, the gorgeous palaces, The solemn temples, the great globe itself, Yea, all which it inherit, shall dissolve And, like this insubstantial pageant faded, Leave not a rack behind. We are such stuff As dreams are made on, and our little life Is rounded with a sleep."

—William Shakespeare, The Tempest